The Moderator

Dwight Kopp

The Moderator

Copyright © 2013 Dwight Kopp

ISBN 978-0-9895853-1-6

Cover Design by Zach Bush.

For series updates, check out the author's Facebook page or visit his website at www.dwightkopp.com.

For Doe

Prolog

Lancaster County, Pennsylvania

Exactly three miles of chain link fence surrounded the Evans, Matthews & Fein research and production facility. The building sat well back from the fence and presented a clean, uncluttered exterior with a tidy brown metal roof. Though it appeared to be only one story when viewed from the road front, it concealed five full subterranean floors. Designated supervisors and security staff serviced each level. Production on the floors changed from year to year at the whim of decision-makers at corporate headquarters somewhere in Georgia.

Corporate recently ordered a complete refurbishing of the entire lower floor known as Fifth Lab. This level alone comprised almost 50,000 square feet of space. Several sections were designed with negative air flow in order to isolate people and other production lines in case of contamination. The big wigs planned to bring in some pretty scary stuff. The floor had all the fixings of a Biohazard Level 4 lab: decon showers, ultraviolet lights, air lines for pressure suits, the works. Preston, a security and software engineer, supervised the refit of all communications and security systems. He worked with a team to ensure a completely unique and isolated network, inaccessible from outside. Anyone who wanted information from this lab had to be inside the room. His blueprints required the floor to be physically separate—not the standard firewall protections he installed elsewhere. Rumor had it that Evans, Matthew & Fein had procured a government contract.

Farwick's pager beeped, and he looked down at the code. A meeting?

He pushed a button and headed to the elevator. It, too, would be decommissioned. A separate elevator was going to be installed on the north end with access only from executive offices. He wasn't sure exactly what they planned to grow down here, but whatever it was, he was sure it was bad.

Farwick stepped out of the elevator and followed the industrial green carpet down to the hallway's end. He paused in front of Sarge's door and straightened his tie. He hated ties and usually undid a top button of his shirt when he wasn't near management.

He walked in. "Hi, Abby. Just got a page from the boss."

She didn't smile. Her eyes were large and she was suddenly busy.

"Something going on?"

She leaned toward her phone and pressed the intercom button. "Sarge, Farwick just came in."

Farwick felt a twinge of something like fear.

"You can go in now." Abby pointed to the conference room in the office suite.

Farwick went into the room and sat down in a swivel chair. He adjusted the arm rests and tried to relax. The room was bare except for a bundle of potted bamboo standing bravely in a soilless water container. The door opened and his boss walked in.

"Hi, Sarge." Farwick sat up.

"Mr. Farwick." Sarge nodded absently in his direction, then set a file on the table.

Mr. Farwick? He never calls me Mr. Farwick, Preston thought. The twinge became more acute.

Sarge pulled a gold pen from his pocket, opened the folder and turned it around so Farwick could read. "Mr. Farwick, this is a notice for termination of employment. It is effective immediately, although you will, of course, be paid up through the end of the month."

Bombshell. Farwick couldn't speak.

"Please sign here at the 'X.'" Sarge set the pen gently down on top of the pink paper.

"What's this? Did I do something wrong?" Farwick asked.

"All I can tell you is your services are no longer required. You'll have to contact the HR department with any further questions."

"Human Resources is in Georgia. What can they tell me that you can't?"

"I'm not at liberty to discuss any details." Sarge glanced at his watch. Other appointments to keep.

Preston Farwick heard the pounding of his own heart in his head. It wasn't possible. His wife was going to fall apart.

"Sign at the 'X' please." Sarge put a carefully manicured finger down on the line. "Right here."

Farwick picked up the pen. His sweaty hands made it slippery. Services no longer required.

Chapter 1

Pennsylvania baked in August.

Ashley Blithe sat in her panties directly beneath the ceiling fan. It was too hot to wear real clothing. She pulled her blond hair into a high, sloppy bun to keep it off her neck. Their house had only two window air conditioners. One in the living room, one in her dad's office. All her friends' homes boasted central air. But her dad was a pastor, and pastors didn't have that kind of money. Ashley's friends never visited their home anyway. High school freshmen generally preferred the mall.

A paltry breeze stirred her bedroom sheers but did nothing for the heat. She flicked on her computer and studied her legs. There wasn't much of a tan line. Just a few freckles and some pink to show where her shorts stopped. Bronzed skin was a pipe dream for a fair- skinned girl like her.

Ashley logged on to the first of two addresses she had gotten from a friend at church. Officially, Darren Firth was her sister's friend. Ashley studied the screen. This was new. The login screen was black and directed her to an onion router. She had heard about these from her brainy friend, Chase. He made it all sound very cloak-and-dagger. Something about hiding what a computer was doing from others by anonymizing its IP address. She had glazed over and didn't remember much else.

Ashley followed the on-screen directions to set up a virtual private network on her computer. Done. Now what?

She typed in the next website address from the paper. The computer seemed to be moving slower. Maybe it was just her imagination. A screen popped up prompting Ashley to create a username and password.

User: PK

Password: LETSROCK

Kind of silly, she thought. She'd used it before.

A single window popped up.

Ashley clicked on the field and dropped in a note. *I'm ready to play.* Enter.

Nothing. Ashley waited for a few minutes. The Moderator must be offline. She was about to close out when a message came in.

This is not a game for sissies.

Ashley made a face at the screen. *That's why I'm here. How do I play?*

Offline.

What r u talking about?

I host the contest. I make the rules. You play in real life.

OK. Ashley shrugged.

What's the point of this game?

To win.

NSS. Figured that.

You will be given a different task than other contestants. The first one to complete the task wins the POG.

POG?

Pot of gold.

How will u know when I win?

I will know.

Now u sound creepy.

Yes.

Ashley shivered. No real breeze was coming in the window but she pulled on a shirt anyway. Mildly spooked, she turned back to the screen. Her green eyes glanced suspiciously at the webcam.

How will I know when I win?

Check your rank on my game page. First player to Level 4 is the champ.

What is my task?

First a test.

I hate tests.

Find another player. Give 'em the game paper. No copies. When they log in, you get to play.

How will you know if I don't give the original?

I will know.

What? RU God or something?

Something.

What if they don't want to play?

Choose wisely.

OK. CU later.

Maybe, PK.

Chapter 2

The Moderator clicked "end chat," leaned back in his chair and hummed along with a bar or two of the Chopin in the background.

"Got one," he said.

Chapter 3

Ashley felt cold hands close around her head, covering her eyes. She yelped and jerked herself around.

"You turd." It was Lisa.

"I love you, too. Kinda jumpy aren't you?" She looked down at Ashley's bare legs. "Bad game of poker?"

"Funny. This room is roasting. Where are you going?" Ashley noticed a touch of blue eye-liner.

"Not where I'm going. Where I've *been*. I just got back."

"Daddy let you go out? I thought you were grounded until Thursday?"

"I am. But Daddy is in a meeting or counseling *Deaconess Hansel*," Lisa leaned on the name a bit to give it a sing-song quality. "I knew we'd have some extra time before he came over from church."

Ashley wrinkled her nose. Renee Hansel oversaw the church's donation program to a local food bank. Aside from being the only other person at church who knew almost everything about their family, Renee also served on the Florin School Board. "You think he's sleeping with her?"

"No. He's the pastor, dummy. Guess what I got at the mall?"

"You were at the mall? Why didn't you invite me along?"

"Because you were sitting here in your underpants. That *would* be a little weird." She sighed. "Come on, guess."

Ashley looked at her older sister's face, trying to read the answer. They were close for sisters. Of course they fought occasionally, but since the day their mother went into the psych ward they had banded together to help keep the dark family secret, dark and secret. Mother was back home, but she wasn't exactly better. A psycho mother wouldn't help their social standing. It was bad enough their father had to be a pastor.

"I don't know."

Lisa stood up and locked the door. Then she knelt on the floor in front of Ashley and rolled up the bottom of her T-shirt. A single shining ring of silver rode the edge of her belly button.

Ashley squealed. "You didn't!"

Lisa smiled. "I did."

Ashley's face fell flat. "Did it hurt?"

"Like hell." They both laughed. "Darren asked me to do it." Darren, unlike the sisters, attended Florin High School. Lisa twisted her lips to the side. "I hope he likes it."

"He's going to kill you." Ashley glanced at the window.

"Darren?"

"No, dummy. Daddy."

"He'll never know. When did you last see a pastor's daughter wearing a bikini at a youth group swim party?"

Chapter 4

The last challenge had been easier than he expected. *Make her bleed for you.* That was it. Easy. All he had to do was send The Moderator a picture, and he'd moved up to Level 2.

But The Moderator wanted more.

DIGA had signed up for high stakes, but it was starting to get ridiculous.

He liked the girl well enough, but this was just crazy. DIGA's face was hot, and he felt a buzzing between his ears.

No thanks. I'm not playing anymore. He wanted to opt out.

The Moderator answered.

DIGA slammed the lid on his laptop and shoved it away. In spite of himself, he felt tears stinging the corners of his eyes. The Moderator knew.

How could he have discovered? No one knew. No one.

DIGA stood and paced his room. He stared at the posters of competitive swimmers on his wall. Famous, strong Olympians. Men with sculpted shoulders and thin legs. His hands trembled. No. No. No, he repeated to himself. I could just deny it, he thought. Maybe I could just laugh it off, but he knows.

The Moderator knows.

And The Moderator would want something. The Moderator always wanted something.

Chapter 5

Ashley stared at the moving van just up from the corner across the street. A black couple walked in and out of the sweltering van, hauling boxes and lamps and bookshelves. She should go help them. A pastor's daughter should go help them. Which was precisely why she stood rooted at the window watching the newcomers carry their own boxes in the heat.

Her dad had spoken with the realtor. The realtor, of course, was a member. She overheard them whispering. Apparently the new family was Islamic. Her father said something about visiting them anyway. When they were settled. After all, they were neighbors. But she had heard her father talk about Muslims before, how they were planning to take over this country, how they talk about peace but their Allah was all about blood and jihad.

She determined she should beat him over there. Wouldn't that just cause a holy scandal among the old choir ladies? The pastor's daughter hanging out with an Islamic family. Besides, she didn't know what jihad was, and she didn't care.

Ashley smiled and let the curtain drop. They didn't look that old. Maybe he had been hired to work at the new wire factory on the edge of town. She walked outside, stepped out of the hot shade from the mammoth pin oak trees and crossed the street.

The man went inside with a box and his wife was struggling to slide what looked like a hope chest toward the back of the moving van. Ashley bit her bottom lip, then walked quickly up the loading ramp and stood there.

"Hi. Can I help you with that?"

The woman looked up. She didn't look like a Muslim. Whatever that was supposed to look like.

"Well, I hate to give away the opportunity to wrestle large objects by myself in heat like this, but since you offered."

Ashley laughed. She was funny. Ashley walked forward and grabbed a handle on the near side of the trunk. "I'm Ashley Blithe," she said. "I live just over there in the rectory. My dad's the pastor."

The woman stood up, stretched her back and offered Ashley her hand. "I'm Rosalyn. Nice to meet you."

No mention of her religion. But then, what did she expect: *Hi my name is Rosalyn and I'm a Muslim*?

They went back to the trunk. Rosalyn made some comment about her husband collecting way too many boring books.

"Is he getting a job at the wire factory?"

"Oh no, honey. Though he might like that better some days. My husband works in Philadelphia. He'll take the train to work. Kind of a long commute, but the neighborhoods are better around here."

"What does he do there?"

"He's a teaching doctor at Temple University."

"Oh, I see." Ashley was embarrassed.

"What do we have here, Rosalyn? Have you already made slaves of neighborhood children?"

Ashley turned to see a man standing on the loading ramp. His arms were folded and a scolding white smile played across his face.

"As a matter of fact, this young lady is a volunteer or a sucker. I'm not sure which, yet." Rosalyn laughed easily. "Ashley, this is my husband, Adam."

"Hi. Nice to meet you." Ashley bit her bottom lip and shook his hand. She had learned all about the art of mix and mingle from her father. "I'm sorry. You'll have to give me your last name. My dad won't want me to call you Rosalyn and Adam."

"Of course. You can call us Dr. and Mrs. Faraj."

"Dr. and Mrs. Faraj."

"That's right."

Ashley helped the neighbors haul in the last few pieces of furniture. She was hot and tired and irritated at herself for coming over to help in the first place. Now she would definitely need a shower. Still, she couldn't think of a way to duck out after having already offered to help. Thankfully, they were near the end by the time she showed up.

"Thanks for your help, Ashley. Can I get you something to drink?"

"No thanks, I should head home. Dad's probably wondering where I got to."

"It is just as well. I'm not sure which box has the glasses." Rosalyn laughed at herself.

Ashley left them to fold furniture blankets and headed home by way of larger pools of shade on the sidewalk. Her mother stood at the kitchen counter stirring noodles from a box for supper and her father lay on the living room floor with a pillow tucked under his head.

"Where were you?" He spoke without opening his eyes. "You were supposed to be finishing up your homework."

"Just saying hello to our new neighbors," Ashley said. She knew this was going to bother him.

"Which neighbors?" His eyes stayed closed.

"The ones who bought Martha Crattsberry's house." Ashley went for the fridge to find something to quench her thirst.

"Don't spoil your supper." Ashley's mother never liked it when she helped herself.

Ashley just rolled her eyes and ignored her.

"I really wish you told us where you were going. Remember, the world is not a safe place for little girls," her dad said.

Same old story. Ashley sighed and walked past him toward the stairs with her water glass. Their icemaker didn't work, but at least the water was cold. She looked at his closed eyes, sneered and gave him the finger. "Okay, dad."

Upstairs, she closed her bedroom door and locked it. Ashley was about to turn on the computer again when she remembered she wasn't going to be able to play the game she wanted to play until she found someone else to join.

She turned on her fan. For once it actually seemed to work. Anything would feel better than the inside of that moving van.

For a while Ashley considered handing off the paper to Lisa. Ashley watched fan blades spinning above her and decided against it. She didn't want Lisa to know about the game. She would hand it off to someone at school.

For now, it would be her secret.

Chapter 6

Sutherland Hall students came from all over the world. Half of them actually lived in the residential complex and the rest commuted from surrounding areas. The school had a reputation as one of the best college preparatory schools on the East Coast. For years Ashley wondered exactly how her parents afforded tuition. They didn't even own their own house. The church owned their home and didn't waste much time on its upkeep.

Though their congregation was small, membership was composed almost entirely of men and women of wealth or position, or both. One of these men was a board member at Sutherland Hall and pulled a few strings so significant scholarship money was made available to Ashley and Lisa. Her parents weren't much interested in the education the school offered, but they did get considerable mileage out of the prestige their attendance afforded the family. "Social-connections" was a game her family played carefully. Sutherland Hall offered status; Florin High did not.

Dunrobin Library crouched like some gothic leftover behind a massive beech tree and an assortment of ancient yews. The yews were especially hideous and their association with the campus didn't endear them to Ashley. *Taxus baccata*, according to her Latin teacher.

Ashley skirted the largest overgrown yew and entered the library through a side door. Ninth grade was the first year her day started with a study hall. After she checked in for homeroom, she usually skipped over to Dunrobin Library where she could always sweet talk the secretary into sharing a cup of coffee.

The standard issue Sutherland tartan and blazer did nothing to keep out the wind, and on cold days, coffee felt especially nice. On a blazing day in late August the coffee was just another something she knew her father wouldn't allow.

Ashley dumped her backpack next to a mahogany table and went for her coffee. She figured it would be easy enough to find another player here. Girls who came to the library in the morning didn't have much to do, and most were looking for adventure. Not exactly a place one would peg as a hangout for bad girls, but it happened to provide a vantage point for watching boys on their way to a public school a few blocks down the street. The public school's preseason athletic camps opened that week.

Sutherland Hall had already started class. It was one of the many drawbacks to a preppy private education. Almost year-round school.

"Hi, Jasmín." Ashley patted the chair beside her. "Join me?"

"Sure." Jasmín sat down, sneaked Ashely's coffee and took a sip. "Yuk. How many sugars do you put in there?"

"Four."

"You're crazy."

"Probably, but it is the only way I can stand the stuff."

"I thought you liked coffee. You're always drinking it."

"Can't stand it, really, but I like the *idea* of coffee."

Jasmín laughed and reached for the paper Ashley was holding. "What's that?"

Ashley held it away from her. "Nothing."

"Some kind of a love note?"

"Not exactly. It's a game."

Jasmín's eyes narrowed. "What game?"

"It is kind of an online game you play offline."

"Would I like it?"

"Yes. I think so, but your parents would freak."

"Since when do we care? Besides, I only see my parents on term breaks."

"Can you keep a secret?"

Jasmín looked cross. "What do you think?"

Ashley glanced around briefly before sliding the game paper across the table. "Just follow the directions. If you want in, you have to pass a test."

Chapter 7

Jasmín could keep a secret.

Ashley knew that for a fact. Ashley's mom had been acting weird for weeks, lying in bed all day, never doing her hair. Laundry collected in large piles around the house. Lisa finally made her first disastrous attempt at doing something about it. The resulting suds left a slippery film on the laundry room floor for days. Eventually they talked their dad into taking care of the laundry. They washed what they needed, learned how to make a few simple meals. They managed, and their father just kept on pretending everything was okay.

But it wasn't okay. Their mom was wack. Large, unhappy circles became so pronounced the sisters referred to her as the "raccoon" when she wasn't around. Their father never seemed to catch on and it served as a handy way of talking about her in front of him.

As a rule they didn't talk much with their parents, but it only got worse after she got sick. They inhabited the same space, but the tension and silence between them seemed to fill the whole house. Lisa spent more time at her boyfriend's place which, thankfully, was an easy walk away. Sometimes Ashley would join them. Most of the time she hid in her room.

Then it got worse.

Ashley still suffered night terrors. At those times, the evil trapped up in her mother's head seemed to fill the whole house, like a haunting. Evil prowled freely. Unfettered by light or day or sanity. Ashley would see her mother's wide, unblinking eyes, feel her clammy hands and face, hear the strange wheezing sounds that should have been regular breathing.

Ashley tried not to care about her mother. They weren't the kind of people most kids hoped for as parents. Distant, cold, religious and preoccupied. But seeing her mother lying on the kitchen floor in a nightgown caked with vomit awakened a blind rage against her dad for standing by and letting his wife go off the deep end.

It was then Ashley first daydreamed about killing the man. At first, she tried to shake the images that came into her mind, but eventually she just let them run wild. Sometimes she would sit at the dinner table and just let it come. He would sit right across from her, making painful attempts at conversation. Ashley would smile and nod and hate him out loud in her mind.

Her mother had gone to a psychiatric hospital for a few days. Short enough not to arouse the suspicions of the nosey church ladies. That was why Renee Hansel knew so much about them. She worked at the hospital. Renee was a psychologist *and* a little too friendly, in her opinion.

It wasn't just about her mother. Every Sunday after that, Ashley would sit in the same place in church and listen to her father preach. And every Sunday she would pick at the bits of skin around her fingernails until they bled. She could hardly stand the pretense.

Jasmín found out about their mother. Actually, she told Jasmín. The need to talk to someone not in her family was too overwhelming. She had chosen well. Jasmín listened and kept it to herself.

The fact that Ashley once walked in on Jasmín and Mr. Carson, the field hockey coach, committing personal fouls didn't hurt. It also didn't hurt that Jasmín happened to be somehow related to the King of Spain, though Jasmín never talked about it. Still, Ashley liked to believe that Jasmín Borbón was just a good friend, and good friends keep secrets.

Chapter 8

DIGA sat facing his computer screen and realized his approach would have to be more direct. He didn't feel inspired; he felt sick. The Moderator was forcing him up to Level 3.

He fumbled around in his desk drawer until he found a working pen and a blank sheet of paper. It wasn't supposed to look like his handwriting. He'd seen the movies. So he wrote a few lines in a feminine cursive. DIGA crumpled up the paper and then pulled out a fresh sheet and arranged another piece of lined paper underneath to keep his sentences straight. No luck. Couldn't see through well enough.

One step at a time, he told himself. Keep The Moderator happy.

He wrote three lines on the paper.

I know all about you.

You're ugly.

I hate you.

They seemed ridiculous to him. She probably wouldn't take them seriously anyway. One of the lines came from The Moderator. He added two of his own. DIGA folded the paper and stuffed it into an envelope. Would she take it as a joke? He peeled the backing off the no-lick flap and pressed it into place. Rummaging again in his drawer he found an alphabet stencil buried since grade school. The letter size was perfect, and he carefully addressed the envelope. No return address. He stole a stamp from his father's desk.

DIGA tucked the envelope into his shorts pocket before he left the house. He fought his bike from between the garden tractor and the garage wall. Evening lengthened the shadows and the breeze cooled his face. Try not to think, he told himself. But he'd been able to do nothing else since he was discovered. Questions chased themselves a round in his head. Nothing ever resolved. He slept badly. When he did sleep, dreams tormented him. Lines of swimmers at the starting block, pointing fingers and laughing. He tried to shake the image from his mind. A few people were out in their gardens, but most had retreated to their climate-controlled living rooms.

DIGA followed the perimeter of the town, keeping to the most deserted roads. He wouldn't make it back before sunset. He needed to get the letter to a post box one town over. It had to be in the mail tomorrow. It was only five miles, but a couple of hills along the way would make for a workout. Exercise usually helped him relax. Not today.

Chapter 9

Ashley typed the address to link up with The Moderator. She remembered to lock her door this time. Not that it mattered. Lisa was out with her boyfriend, and her parents never came up here.

She typed in the dialogue box.

I think I've found a new player. Did I pass the test?

Ashley waited.

Finally, The Moderator started typing. She could feel excitement rising. The reply arrived and her computer dinged.

Not yet, PK.

Chapter 10

Rosalyn Faraj worked in her kitchen. Boxes crowded in piles in just about every corner, but she'd managed to find the basic dishes and a few necessary pots and pans. It felt good to be cooking in her own kitchen again. She glanced over at Jared, who sat hunched over a math book at the kitchen bar.

"How's it going?"

"Okay, I guess. I've only got a few more problems. Then I'll be done, I think."

"No. I mean school. What are your classes like? Meet anyone?"

"Not sure, really. There sure are a whole bunch of white faces." He chuckled. "Sure ain't Philly."

"Sure *isn't* Philly." She waved a spatula in his direction.

"That either. Most of the kids seem friendly enough, I guess. Chemistry is going to be tough."

"Did you see the football coach?" Rosalyn strained noodles through a colander, raising a cloud of steam.

"Yes. He wasn't happy about me joining the team because I missed two weeks of camp." Jared circled the answer on his paper and closed his book. "He said I could stop by tomorrow, and he'd take a look. He'll probably give most of the playing time to guys who busted their—"

"Stop right there. Don't even think about getting a potty mouth on me."

"I was *going* to say, 'busted their behinds' at camp."

"Well, you just go out there and give your best effort. Support the team, and I'm sure the coach will play you when he thinks you've earned it."

"That's the plan." Jared slid off the bar stool and gathered up his books. "What time is Dad getting home?"

"Not sure. I think he'll be here by 6:30 tonight."

Chapter 11

The Moderator opened a browser and logged into his Shodan account. Unlike Google, Shodan would find anything connected to the Internet. He set the filters for the school's city and state, then clicked enter.

A single desk lamp set angular shadows across the uncluttered surface of his desk. The hunter worked methodically. Mechanically. A hint of a smile touched his mouth. It was all so easy.

After a few minutes, the search engine displayed results. The Moderator sifted through the code and found the Sutherland Hall library computer. He typed *AdminPassword* and clicked enter.

Nothing.

He tried /Password1/.

"Bingo." He stared at the admin screen for the library catalog and user system. "Don't forget to change your password," he whispered.

He pulled up the library user list and saved a copy to his desktop.

He reached for the glass on his desk and took a sip. "Now I have you. All of you. Let's do a little research."

Chapter 12

Ashley had known Chase Hikeman since kindergarten. They'd been in the same class until Ashley moved over to Sutherland. Chase had to stand up straight to reach the five foot mark. His round glasses seemed to be constantly slipping because his ears didn't hold them in place. His ears were the reason most kids at Florin High gave no consideration to Chase. But unlike most squirrely teenagers, Chase had something going for him: He was smart, and he knew it. As a result, he could ignore the rude comments and snide remarks. Other kids would have been depressed, or self-conscious, or withdrawn. Chase didn't give a rat's ass what others thought about him, which is precisely why Ashley decided to be his friend.

Chase lived across town in the Terraces—a broom factory converted into high-density housing. His mother worked crazy hours, and his dad wasn't in the picture. Chase maintained odd interests. He was a computer geek of sorts, but he always had some other project going that took them to unusual places. At fourteen, he was one of the few boys Ashley knew who wasn't addicted to video games, and he was the only boy she knew who could maintain what sounded like intelligent conversation with just about any adult he encountered.

Perhaps most of all, Ashley liked hanging with someone who wasn't connected with her family or school in any way. Chase was a breath of fresh air. Even in August.

As usual, Ashley met Chase on Saturday morning at the park under the gigantic leaves of the sycamore. She knew he liked her. He told her once that he liked her figure. She wasn't interested in him that way, but she didn't mind the attention. The problem with attending an all-girls school was that it had way too many girls. And the girls Ashley hung out with almost always talked about clothes and boys. Chase's world interested her.

"I think I've found something." Chase didn't even bother to say hello.

"What do you mean?" Ashley fell into step beside him. "Where are we going?"

"Farther down Barbara Street." He paused at a break in the trees and pointed back across the park to a red brick warehouse several blocks away. "That's Jay's Pub."

Chase bumped his glasses back in place. "The pub has a catacomb in the basement with a vaulted arched ceiling made entirely of stone."

"I know. I've been down there. It's a restaurant now, remember?"

"No kidding." The idea stopped Chase. "Is it nice?"

"I guess. Expensive, I think, and kinda weird."

"Weird how?"

"Like a dungeon, I guess."

"Well, I was digging through the archives in the library and found an old map. The map showed that those catacombs extended across town and down toward the creek." He pointed again to the bottom of a short hill where the sidewalk ended at a main road.

The road crossed a creek before heading out of town.

"So?"

"So, I think it is still here."

They continued walking until they stood across the street from a stone building divided into apartments that Chase's mom could never dream of affording.

"What do you mean still here? Still where?"

"Right under that house."

"So you're just going to go up and knock on the door and ask to see their basement."

"No. I was hoping you would do that."

"Not a chance, Chase."

"I thought you might say that." He took her by the hand and led her across the street. "Follow me."

Chase took Ashley to the bottom of the hill where they could peer into the backyard of the stone building. The backyard sloped downhill until it ran into thin, messy woods lining the winding creek.

"I don't see anything," Ashley said. "You?"

"What I don't see is a dog. That's good. What I do see is a way into the lower level right over there." He pointed to a set of barn-style doors that opened into a daylight basement. "What are you doing tonight?"

"Are you asking me on a date?"

Chase smiled. "Maybe. Say 11:30?"

"I'm not allowed out after 10."

"I know. Make sure you bring a flashlight."

Chapter 13

Jasmín Borbón lived in the Septa Quad of girls' dorms. Most observers found the dorms to be excellent examples of American Colonial architecture. The girls just thought they were old and nasty. After field hockey practice, Jasmín logged on from her phone. She followed the directions on the single slip of paper Ashley gave her.

Then she set up her login:

User: *Princess*

Password: *Borbón*

Jasmín liked to keep things simple. Adults could be so paranoid about Internet security. She twisted a strand of hair while she waited. She heard a noise in the hallway and slipped the phone under her pillow just as the senior resident assistant came in.

"Thanks for knocking." Jasmín's smile held no pleasure.

"How am I ever going to catch you in the act if I always warn you when I'm about to come in?"

"You're right." Jasmín sighed. "In fact, you better check for the boys I've hidden under my bed."

"Good night, Jasmín." The RA flashed a sarcastic smile and flicked off the light on her way out.

Jasmín resisted the temptation to turn the light back on, but instead slid under her sheets and grabbed the phone.

She punched the power on and sat staring at her first message from The Moderator:

Jasmín, I've been waiting.

How did he know my name? Jasmín wondered. Probably got it from Ashley. She typed:

Gr8. What's the game? She waited.

First a rule. Then two tests.

OK.

Rule: Never talk about the game.

Fine.

Test 1: Mail the paper.

The Moderator gave Jasmín a post office box address somewhere in Wisconsin.

Test 2?

First complete test one.

Chapter 14

Ashley met Chase by the park and they walked the long way around to get back to the property by the creek. They both wore dark clothing. Rain had come through and cooled the temperature a bit. Still Ashley's black hoodie felt overly warm.

"I hope you know what you're doing," Ashley said.

"You didn't have to come."

"Of course, I did."

The two ducked into the woods and followed the creek toward the back side of the house. The mosquitoes were thick and stung Ashley's legs through the back of her jeans.

They sneaked across the parking lot to the barnlike doors and ducked in through one that hung ajar. They stood in the dark, afraid to turn on their flashlight when a metallic buzzer sounded right beside them. Chase's clammy hand clamped over her mouth, stifling a cry.

"It's a clothes' dryer. Let's get moving before someone comes down here." Ashley turned to leave.

"Wait, we need to go back that way and see if there's an access point," Chase said.

The two crept around the log-hewn posts toward another section of the basement. Chase turned on his flash light, but shielded the lens. He panned the light across the back wall. A rotting green door sagged on black strap hinges and the two scuttled toward it.

Somewhere behind them, they could hear the sound of footsteps coming down from the main house above. "Get inside!" Chase commanded.

The door scraped on gravel as she pulled it aside. The two of them tumbled into the darkness of the tunnel beyond.

Chapter 15

The van emblazoned with a yellow "school students" sign stopped at the curb, hazard lights flashing. Theirs was the last stop. Lisa couldn't wait to change out of her plaid tartan kilt. Attending an all-girls school was bad enough, but the kilt positively advertised it to the world. Their driver insisted on stopping a full two blocks from their house.

The girls walked home together.

"I'm starving," Ashley said.

"You're always starving."

"I'm not starving after I eat."

Lisa rolled her eyes. "You have a lot of homework?"

"Not really, just Latin."

"Now there's a truly practical subject. Study a language that almost no one speaks," Lisa said.

"I know, right?"

Lisa stopped at the mailbox and Ashley walked inside to make a sandwich.

Lisa picked absently through the letters. Between the neon green burn-ban notice from the borough and several chunky credit card offers was a square pink envelope bearing her name. She stopped walking. A letter for her. Strange. Lisa slid the letter into the outside pocket of her tartan, shifted the shoulder strap of her bag and kept walking. She had never received an actual letter before. Didn't know people still did that.

Lisa dropped her bag inside the door and walked upstairs to change. She could open the letter in her room.

Chapter 16

Pastor Blithe slept on the couch in his home office. He couldn't stand his wife's restless insomnia. Elizabeth Blithe sat alone in her room staring at the black window pane, waiting for the eyes to look in again. Her fingers picked relentlessly at the frayed edge of her housecoat. She knew they would come, knew they would peer into the room as soon as she wasn't watching.

Elizabeth pulled the robe tighter around her. Then she heard it again. Voices in her head. It was like a recorded laughter played at a slow speed. Strange and guttural and terrifying. She pressed her hands over her ears and tried to scream. Terror choked her voice into a strange hissing noise. The hissing added to the terror swirling around her. She stumbled from her place on the bed to the closet. Something was moving in her room now. A black shape walking toward her, arms outstretched. Evil face smiling at her. It came closer. Elizabeth lashed out at the shape, finally finding a vent.

Elizabeth fought against it. Kicking, scratching, fighting.

Reluctantly it went away. She closed her eyes. Still the laughter. Still the evil smile. She pushed her hands back over her ears to drown out the sound and pressed herself into the corner by the closet, sliding down into a fetal position against the wall.

Chapter 17

Ashley looked across the table at Lisa. Her sister's face and neck were covered with scratches. A green bruise shadowed the underside of Lisa's chin. Marks from another night spent trying to keep their mother sane.

"I told you to stay out of there," Ashley whispered. "She isn't safe."

"But she was crying. She was so afraid." Lisa touched her own face gently.

Phillip looked up from rehearsing his sermon notes. His face flashed concern. Then panic. Then the mask returned. "You're not feeling well today. Why don't you stay home from service and get some rest?"

Ashley poured milk over her cereal and carried her bowl into the living room to watch the news. She didn't want to sit at the table with her father. She didn't want to pretend that nothing happened the night before. She sat in the large wing back chair that kept her father from seeing her own tears.

"You're not allowed to eat in the living room," her dad called from the kitchen table.

Ashley mouthed something else, but aloud she said, "I'll be careful."

She barely tasted the cereal.

Chapter 18

Chase pushed his glasses into place and knocked on the door of the rectory, which, with the church, took up the corner of the block. The rectory itself was surrounded by a grand expanse of green grass nicely kept. Chase loved the look of all that grass. He determined that one day he would live in a house with a yard. He allowed himself a moment of regret at his family's financial state.

The door finally opened just a crack and Lisa peeked out.

"Oh, it's you. Hang on a minute. I'll get Ashley."

Chase sat down on the flagstone step and pulled at a weed growing up from a crack in the mortar.

"Hi, Chase." Ashley was behind him.

"You know," he held out the thistle, "that tiny bit of root I didn't get will grow again. That's why you need to get the whole root on a weed. Poison works better. It goes systemic in the plant and –"

"Chase, I really don't have time to hang out today. I've got to finish my Latin homework."

"Right. 'Carpe diem' and all that."

Ashley chuckled. "What do you want, Chase? You here to teach me about weeding?"

"No." Chase looked around suspiciously. "Can we walk the block?"

"Chase, I have to finish my homework."

"This is more important than Latin."

"Perfect. Let's go."

Ashley pulled the door shut behind her. She wore a simple T-shirt over a pair of tight athletic shorts that quickly had Chase's attention.

"Focus, Chase."

Chase made eye contact again. "Call of the wild." A smirk.

"Very funny."

They headed down the sidewalk. Chase whispered, "About our trip yesterday to the underground chamber."

"What about it? You suddenly grew a conscience?"

"I just think we need to keep it private." Chase's face was serious.

"Why? What's the big deal?"

"Well, you know how people are. All it takes would be a couple of stupid kids getting in there, decorating the wall with pseudo satanic nonsense and the whole place would be a mess."

"So?"

"So we need to keep a lid on it. Don't talk to anyone about it."

"Chase, have you forgotten that I'm a girl?"

Chase stopped, pushed his glasses and looked at her directly in the face. "What's your point?"

"You happen to be the only person I know who might enjoy sneaking into another person's house to find hidden underground rooms."

"You'll have to admit it was pretty amazing. The hallway leading into it must have been almost thirty feet long."

"Chase. I don't have any friends that would care about it. You care because you're weird and you like that stuff."

Chase looked down. She was the only one who could hurt his feelings, and she seemed to notice.

"Look. I like weird, but the rest of my friends wouldn't be interested."

"Anyway," Chase sighed, "keep it to yourself?"

"Okay. No problem. Are you planning to go back?"

"No," Chase said. "I don't want to risk someone else following me and finding it." He paused, trying to think of a way to help her understand. "It's a piece of history, you know."

"Chase, it is a room made out of stone. It happens to be underground. The tenants who live there probably don't even know about it."

"Don't you see? The catacombs under Florin were used to smuggle booze during Prohibition. Before that, they were way-stations in the underground railroad."

"No kidding." She hadn't thought about the other people who might have been in there. "Okay. Deal. I'll keep it a secret."

"Promise?" Chase crossed his arms.

"I promise."

Chapter 19

Jared Faraj walked into the backyard and looked around. It wasn't wide, but it was deep enough. He threw the football up overhead and watched it spiral neatly down again into his hands. Mismatched fences marked the perimeter of their backyard. The end opposite the house opened onto an alley.

Jared waited for his dad to finish the Asr prayer. He knew his dad wanted him to join, but Jared wasn't sure about all that and was glad his dad gave him space to figure out his own questions about God. Of course, Jared could recite the rak'a in his sleep. He even owned a prayer rug.

Some Muslims completed their daily prayers regardless of where they were. Adam Faraj determined he would be faithful without embarrassing anyone. But at home, he could pray in his own way. Facing east.

Jared admired his father. He didn't care what the rest of the world thought about Muslims. He would wait for him.

Chapter 20

The Moderator drank his whiskey neat.

"Perfect," he said to no one. He was alone except for a slumbering brute of a German shepherd sprawled in front of the doorway.

The Moderator swept his hands gently across the keyboard before typing. A half smile played across the corner of his mouth. "Come to papa."

The dog shuffled up from her spot and stood at his elbow. "Not you, Cookie." He patted her head. "Lay down." The shepherd yawned and settled herself at the edge of his chair, waiting for more attention.

Her master leaned back and studied the screen. "Cookie, move." He turned and pulled out a drawer. One file tab for every player. 8male, Abyssmal, DIGA, PK, Princess, Sillygirl3 and others.

Twelve fishes, 12 files. He now had all his game papers back. Or at least they were sitting in a post office box a thousand miles away.

Chapter 21

Lisa sat on the floor with her legs crossed. A children's coloring book lay open before her. She knew 17-year-olds didn't usually color, but she didn't care. She gave the fairy princess golden hair and a perfect green dress. Sometimes coloring helped. Her colored pencils lay like a pile of pick-up sticks next to her. All the points were dull. Lisa reached for her pencil sharpener and stared at it. Her toes curled underneath her, and she chewed on the inside of her mouth.

She pulled the letter from her pocket and stared at the words again.

I know all about you.

You're ugly.

I hate you.

She had the words memorized but she liked to stare at them, think about them, practice hating herself. She felt something fog up her mind, the same fog that shut her down in math class when the teacher called her out. Stupid, stupid, stupid. The voice repeated itself. Her own voice joined the sound of others in her head.

Lisa's fingers reached for the tiny eyeglass screwdriver hanging from a tub chain around her neck. She would need to let the stupid out again. She would need to let the ugly out. Maybe this time bleeding would make her feel better. Her fingers worked out the dull, silver blade from the pencil sharpener.

She set the blade on the picture of her fairy princess and pulled off her socks. It was better there. It hurt more on her feet.

And no one would notice.

Chapter 22

The woman working the dispatch listened to the caller on the other end. She tapped a few notes into the computer and relayed them to the officer on duty.

Officer Dixon closed the door of his police cruiser. He had just picked up a coffee and a banana from a local supermarket. If he stopped in before the 10 a.m., the coffee still tasted decent. He read the message on the dashboard monitor.

"What the hell?" He settled the coffee into his cup holder and threw the banana onto the seat beside him. Officer Dixon recently got one of the new turbocharged 3.5-liter V-6 interceptors. A perk of no longer being the low man on the totem pole. The cruiser boasted all the bells and whistles and enough get-up-and-go to stave off the doldrums of a boring beat.

He punched it up a bit because traffic was thin, but he didn't turn on the lights. It might be considered a bit melodramatic to use the lights when responding to a call about another dead cat.

Dixon arrived at the address and found an elderly woman sitting on her porch holding an embroidered cloth handkerchief.

"Good morning ma'am." Dixon walked up onto the porch. "Are you Mrs. Eshelman?"

"Yes. Thank you for coming. I have no idea why someone would do this."

"I'm sorry. Can you show me?"

"No. I can't go back there again. She's in the alley behind the house. Just follow the sidewalk back."

"Thank you. I'll go have a look." Dixon turned to go, but the old lady called out to him again.

"Young man. Would you please cut her down for me? I didn't have the heart."

Dixon found the cat hanging from its neck on a length of forty-pound fishing line. It ran over top of a power line, suspending the cat almost 15 feet in the air.

He squinted to follow the line down the other side.

Dixon pulled out a knife and cut the fishing line where it had been tied off to a chain-link fence.

Chapter 23

"Why did you tell him my name?" Jasmín folded her arms.

"Tell who your name?" Ashley smiled. "Another guy after you?"

"Stop, I'm serious."

"What are you talking about?"

"You know. What I'm not supposed to talk about."

"No. I don't know."

"The game, silly."

"What game? What guy?"

Jasmín leaned closer and whispered, "The Moderator."

Ashley made a face. "I *didn't* tell him your name."

"Yeah. Okay." Jasmín said.

"No, really." Ashley racked her brain. Suddenly she couldn't remember for sure.

"I'm supposed to believe he just pulled that out of thin air?" Jasmín picked up her backpack. "I'm going to class."

Ashley felt sick.

Chapter 24

Ashley logged on at 9:30 p.m. Her parents were downstairs getting ready for bed. Her head ached from clenching her jaw. Most evenings were like that.

She typed in her password and opened a dialog box.

Can I play now?

Yes.

It's about time. Ashley thought. *How did you find out her name?*

Whose name?

Jasmín.

I have my ways. Are you ready to play?

Yes.

Are you feeling angry?

Yes. How did you know?

I have my ways.

Who do you hate?

Everyone. Except my sister and Chase. Why?

I'm coming up with a challenge.

Challenge?

Yes. The player who completes his challenge first wins, remember?

'Her' challenge, Ashley corrected. As soon as she hit send she thought better of it. She probably shouldn't tell him anything personal. Oh well.

A pause. The Moderator was thinking. *Do you have any black neighbors?*

Yes.

How long since they moved in?

Two weeks.

Another pause.

Log in Saturday, and I'll have your game ready.

Why not now?

Patience, PK. Patience.

Chapter 25

"It is all about triangulation." The teenager sat down on the edge of the pool next to Officer Dixon. Dixon opened his pool to the neighbors whenever he was home. It was his personal outreach program and it kept the local kids on his team. Not too many officers lived in the same area where they ran their beat.

"What do you mean triangulation?" Dixon looked over at the kid from his pool chair. A couple of bikini clad seniors from Florin High lay in the sun on the far side of the pool deck.

"Triangulation, you know? If you want to locate a specific point, all you need are three different readings on a seismograph. Three readings give you three circles. Where the circles intersect is the epicenter."

"Okay, Ralph, I get that. I do remember something from my high school science class. What does that have to do with online stalkers?"

Ralph pulled a banana-yellow swim cap down over his uncombed mass of curls. "It is kind of cool, really. The stalker starts by getting a couple of data points. They're insignificant, you know, but they're usually enough."

"Give me a data point" Dixon said.

"Name, gender, location, school colors."

"Kids actually give that information out?"

"Sure. Of course most don't know they're doing it. Sometimes data is mined in the same way interest-based advertising sends you the advertisements for a product you were just looking at."

"How do they get a data point from that?"

"Obviously if someone on the net is looking at purses, the stalker can assume it is a girl. Well, usually anyway." Ralph chuckled.

"How does a stalker get someone else's cookies?"

"Only the website that gives the cookie can read it. So a stalker might set up a false business that caters to the kind of person he wants to track. You don't actually have to buy anything in order to leave personal data. Window shopping is a dead giveaway."

"How does a stalker know who the computer belongs to that is tracking the product?"

"What do they teach you at cop school anyway?" Ralph shook his head in wonder. "There are companies online who offer geolocation services." Ralph saw only a blank stare. "Geolocation is a service that identifies with reasonable accuracy the location of an IP address. Sometimes they can even give you the town. It is a pretty good deal for businesses online who want to locate their customer base. That data could save them millions if they want to set up a distribution center somewhere. If they can get their distribution center closer to the bulk of their customers, they'll be able to save the difference on shipping, or charge a lower price."

"Makes sense until that information falls into the wrong hands. Then the bad guy puts that information with what he knows and –"

"Exactly. A town, plus school colors, and a stalker has just narrowed down his search quite a bit. I think it's like a game for them."

"Do all the kids know this stuff?" Dixon asked.

"Some do. Most don't really care. No one really thinks he's going to get targeted."

Chapter 26

Jasmín liked to sit in the recesses of Dunrobin Library, which included study cubicles in just about every section. She entered the password to the building's wi-fi. Students were forbidden to use the system, but most of her friends knew the code.

Funny how adults think kids are clueless, Jasmín thought.

She logged on to the game site from her phone, typed 'hello' to The Moderator, and waited.

The Moderator took his time writing back. She had almost given up when a single line appeared on the screen.

Jasmín, you broke a rule.

What?

She told me.

Who?

Guess.

Ashley?

You talked about the game.

OMG.

She told me everything.

WTF? Angry tears stung her eyes. "What a b—"

Everything. You will have to pay a penalty for breaking a rule.

A penalty? Why?

To prove I can trust you.

*U *can* trust me.*

Prove it.

Chapter 27

I don't want to play anymore.

2 L8 4 U.

I'm not coming back. DIGA wanted out.

Can you afford to not *play?*

Go to hell.

You have 24 hours to reconsider.

DIGA shuddered with anger. He turned off the computer and pulled the plug out of the wall. He wanted to scream at someone, to hurt someone. He wanted to start over.

Too late.

Their house was almost 4,000 square feet. His parents' master suite occupied more than half of the second floor, but they were never in there together. In fact, they were almost never home. DIGA left his room and paced restlessly around the house. Panic followed him everywhere he went. He needed to hide.

DIGA went down to the bar in the basement, pulled a bottle off the shelf. He took a hit. His throat burned. DIGA took the bottle back upstairs and slammed the door of his room for effect. No one was home. It didn't matter.

No one cared anyway.

He continued to drink in hopes of drowning out the noise in his head. He could hear the mocking and the laughter and the red hot sting of shame.

The shame songs everyone sings in grade school. *Darren is gay.* The song played over and over in his mind. K – I – S – S – I – N – G. *Darren is gay.*

He couldn't stand it. He drank some more.

Twenty-four hours to reconsider. If he didn't reconsider, the Moderator would tell the world.

Chapter 28

Officer Dixon sat down across from Chief Gregson's desk.

"So what do you make of all this?" Gregson asked.

"Normally, I wouldn't make anything of it. Not more than a bunch of kids with a pretty sick idea of a practical joke."

"That's a lot of dead cats." Gregson flipped through the file in front of him.

"I wouldn't have thought much of it except for a conversation I had with a friend a couple of townships over who said he's seen a few cats hanging from fishing line. Wondered if it were some kind of gang symbol."

"You think it's gang related?" Gregson looked up at Dixon.

"I don't think so. You remember that planking craze? I don't know where it began, but people all over the world photographed themselves planking and posted the pictures online. I wonder that this isn't something like that here. Pictures of cats hanging from a fishing line are showing up in some pretty weird places."

"Don't kids have anything better to do?" Gregson sighed. "Make sure you bring that along to our meeting with the board Tuesday night. We'll have a projector set up. Make sure you include that in our presentation. Maybe we'll get the funding to make the hire."

"How do you want me to handle this now?"

"Go ahead and call that computer guy. He knows we want to take him on full time, but he might be willing to keep working on a per diem basis. Maybe he can turn up something."

Chapter 29

The Moderator sat staring at the blinking cursor in the dialog box and whistling softly under his breath. Cookie lay sleeping in the doorway as usual. Classical music played softly in the background. PK had just logged on.

This was going to be interesting.

It is Saturday. PK signed in without a greeting. She must be hot about something.

The Moderator pressed his stopwatch. Always make them wait two minutes, he thought. Two minutes should do it.

He directed the music with lazy fingers. One minute. Come to papa. A new song began and his fingers hovered over the keys.

Are you sure you can handle it?

Yes.

Some other gamers are already in play.

How come they have a head start?

I host the contest. I make the rules.

Whatever, she thought. *What is my challenge?*

Make your neighbors move.

Ashley Blithe stared at the words and felt a tingle of excitement.

Which neighbors? The black ones?

Yes.

How?

Should I find someone else who can handle it?

Ashley made a face at the screen. *No. I've got this.*

She knew just what to do. *How will you know when they're gone?*

I'll know.

Right. Do I know you?

Ashley waited but there was no reply on the other end.

Her mind buzzed from a double shot of energy drinks and the room felt cramped. She got up, slipped into a pair of pink flops and hit the sidewalk. No one was out. The sun baked the grass crisp, and thick hot air held the pin oak leaves still in the trees.

She unconsciously avoided the cracks in the concrete as she walked and thought about her mother. She hadn't seen her that day. It seemed the woman almost never got out of bed. It was probably her medicine. The good pastor busied himself at the church office on weekends, preparing his sermons or whatever he did over there. Regardless, he was rarely home. Never there to see his wife lying in bed until noon. Rarely there to see her stumble down to the kitchen to find her next pill. Never there to see her ignore her children.

Ashley spelled out what she thought of him with the rhythm of schoolgirls jumping rope. She remembered the chalk lines Lisa would draw for her on the sidewalk. Those were the days when she could look up and see her mom smiling from the kitchen window while she played hopscotch.

She always liked games.

"Hi, Ashley." The sound of her name shut down the memory. It was Rosalyn Faraj. Ashley was right in front of their house. Rosalyn held a green plastic watering can.

Ashley remembered the game.

Mrs. Faraj kept talking. "Every time I turn around I hear the black-eyed Susans calling for water. "You want something to drink? I found the glasses."

"Sure." Ashley followed her up the stairs. "It is pretty hot out."

"I'm glad you stopped by. My boys are both away today. Dr. Faraj is at the hospital and Jared has some kind of Saturday practice. Their coach doesn't seem to believe in a day off."

"I didn't know you had a son."

Mrs. Faraj stopped and turned around. "I guess you didn't. I just assumed you met at school or something. Yes, Jared is a sophomore."

Ashley was suddenly quiet, and her host noticed. Mrs. Faraj passed her a glass of sun tea. "Everything okay?"

"Yeah, sure." Ashley took a drink of her tea. "It's just I thought maybe it might scare you."

"Scare me? Honey, what are you talking about?" Mrs. Faraj raised her eyebrows.

"Just having a son at the school and all."

"What about the school?" Mrs. Faraj put her glass down and kept looking at her. Ashley made her decision.

"Nothing, really. It's just rumors, I guess." Ashley bit her lip. She imagined the hopscotch lines again. She noticed a kind of shadow pass over Mrs. Faraj's face. One hop at a time, she thought. "Never mind. Dad says gossip is a sin."

Ashley finished her drink. "I'd better be going. Thanks for the tea."

Mrs. Faraj walked her back out to the front porch.

"Well, look who finally decided to show up."

A well-built young man climbed the front steps. "Hi, Mom."

"I thought your coach was never going to let you come home."

The boy just smiled, then gave Ashley a quick once-over. Mrs. Faraj made introductions.

"Jared, this is Ashley. She lives just around the corner." Ashley smiled and gave the boy a wave. He was cute and sweaty. Not that she thought the two often went together.

"It looks like you could use a shower." Mrs. Faraj stared at the tee shirt sticking to her son's muscular frame. "You can hug me later."

"Me too," Ashley added.

Jared laughed easily and walked past them into the house.

"Thanks for coming." Mrs. Faraj watched Ashley walk down the stairs, then called after her. "Remember, if there is anything you think I should know, be sure to stop by."

Ashley just nodded and watched the woman turn back inside.

She walked quickly now. Determined. A skeleton plan formed in her mind as she walked home.

Chapter 30

The board meeting began to fill up with the awkward chatter of Sunday-go-to-church people who met up mid-week. Mr. Kramer, the chairman, glanced at his watch and nodded to the secretary. He cleared his throat a few times and the room got quiet. No one really wanted to be here. Community service looked good on one's lapel, but it was boring as hell.

"We've got quite a few items to go over tonight, so let's begin." Kramer spoke to the board and the few community members who religiously showed up. Most of them were part of the townships old guard. These were the same people who patrolled the sidewalks of the no-light towns and called the police on folks who didn't pick up after their dogs.

Others in attendance included a high school senior who wrote for the local gazette and a handful of police officers.

"We'll begin with the request for a variance by one Melinda VanKhor." The board chair picked up the request and adjusted his glasses. "Ms. VanKhor would like to construct a fence toward the rear of her property. Reason for request is as follows," he was reading from a pink paper. "Apparently, the local dogs keep defecating in her flower beds."

A ripple of laugher touched at the fringes of the room. Kramer removed his glasses and looked out at the audience. "Mr. Snipe." An older man leaned out from his place in the rear of the audience. Kramer continued. "I thought you patrolled that area heavily. Isn't that part of your morning beat?"

The audience flirted with another chuckle. Everyone knew Snipe was a force of overactive citizenry. The township office usually heard from him three to four times per week. He called in folks who were burning yard waste or those who left their cars running when they stepped into the post office.

Kramer didn't give Mr. Snipe the chance to respond. "It isn't your dog littering in Ms. VanKhor's yard, is it?"

Mr. Snipe pretended to be offended, but Kramer moved on. "Any comments on the action?" He paused briefly to glance at the various board members.

Glenda Morrison spoke up from her corner. As the only woman member, she made it a point to get in on the action whenever there was something to do. "I motion we approve the variance and issue Ms. VanKhor a building permit."

Another member seconded the motion.

Mr. Kramer glanced back into the audience and called for Officer Dixon to present the issue of supplemental funding for the hire of a cyber-detective.

Dixon came to the front of the room. Using Ralph's theory of triangulation and a presentation he had spent way too much time preparing, he covered the basics. The predator risk to youth was increasing due to advances in technology; the local police department was ill-equipped to track crimes involving said technology; the police department needed extra funding to hire a cyber-detective. When he finished the presentation, he asked for questions.

Kramer glanced down at his notes. "Officer Dixon, help me understand. A man can learn about our kid's school colors online?"

Dixon shot a 'help-me' look at Chief Gregson in the audience. "Well, Mr. Kramer. It isn't about the school colors; it is about what a potential predator can learn online that allows him to figure out where our children are located."

Kramer wagged his head. Glenda Morrison chimed in again. "Officer Dixon, how often does a child get harmed from someone online?"

"Frequently. Cyber-bullying, for example, has become a huge problem."

"Cyber-what?" Kramer spoke up again.

"Bullying, sir. Name calling, spreading gossip, posting naked or near-naked pictures of other kids."

Kramer let out a burst of air. "Officer Dixon, when I was in grade school people called me toothpick." He sat up in his chair and patted his ample stomach. "As you can see, I healed from that deep trauma and have done rather well for myself."

The gathering laughed openly now, and Kramer rode the wave into his next comment. "I fail to see how we need to allocate another $75,000 for a job to keep track of mean people who may not even reside in our state. It is even possible that these *mean* people may be in another country. Is that correct?"

Dixon fought to recover some kind of momentum. "I suppose that is possible, but—"

"I motion we deny the request for funding." Glenda Morrison jumped in.

The motion was seconded and recorded by the secretary. Dixon sat down, obviously deflated. Chief Gregson leaned over and whispered, "That went well."

"Yeah, it was brilliant."

Chapter 31

Jasmín formulated her plan before she logged on. According to The Moderator, Ashley had already told him everything about her. She wasn't sure of exactly what Ashley had said, but she figured it probably included all the details of her relationship with the field hockey coach. Of course, they weren't 'together' anymore. But, he *was* very handsome and very married. Even with all her connections, Sutherland Hall would never tolerate that.

She thumbed in her password. *I'm here.*

Jasmín waited for The Moderator to come online. It seemed to take him a while. The Moderator probably wasn't working from his phone. Maybe he is an older man who logs in from his office. Maybe he's cute. Jasmín chuckled at the thought. Who knew?

His message blinked onto the screen. *Are you ready to pay your penalty?*

I am. Go ahead. She replied.

The Moderator wanted to know Ashley's greatest fear. If Ashley hadn't betrayed her, she could never have done it. Never.

Jasmín read the words before she clicked send. *Ashley fears the world will discover her mother is a schizophrenic.*

The Moderator seemed to be thinking. Deciding if it were big enough. Finally, his answer came through.

Penalty accepted.

Now what? She asked.

You still want to play the game?

Yes.

Same rules.

Fine.

Who do you hate? He asked.

Right now?

Yes.

She keyed in the name in slowly. *Ashley.*

In order to accomplish your task, you will need to be her friend.

Why?

Friends are more dangerous than enemies.

Jasmín smiled.

Chapter 32

Preston Farwick sat in the crowded bleachers squinting into the setting sun. He wiped his broad, sweating forehead with the palm of his hand before pulling his ball cap back on. He picked up the hotdog he bought at the concession stand and stuffed one end into his mouth. Too bad about the beer. There wasn't a high school stadium in the country that would consider selling beer. He watched the players down in the field. The crowd was electric in the way only a high school football crowd could be.

Preston Farwick didn't care much for football and seated himself at the highest point in the bleachers— far away from the kids and the over-eager cheerleaders, who didn't care about the game either. He enjoyed people-watching, and this was the best place for it.

The opposing team's bleachers bristled with visitors, and the tension was thick. Fans cheered wildly at the slightest provocation, and the game only just started.

Farwick saw Ken Dixon walking up the side stairway. Dixon saw Farwick in the back row and waved to him. Farwick waved back and watched him pick his way around the few other people in the row to get to where he sat.

"Hey, Preston." Dixon shook hands with his friend. "Sorry I'm late. Had to tie up a few loose ends at the office. Too much paper work these days. What ever happened to 'find the bad guy, put him in jail, and go home happy'?"

Preston chuckled and nodded to the seat beside him. "Sit down. Tell me your troubles."

"Yep. I've got a few of those."

Farwick grimaced. "It didn't go well, huh?"

"No. Sorry, Preston."

Farwick thumped the bleacher with his fist. "I've got to get a real job. If my unemployment runs out and I still don't have anything, the wife is going to have my head."

"I tried, but they just don't get it." He gestured vaguely to the bleachers below them. "These kids are more vulnerable than they have ever been, and we are more ill-equipped than we have ever been."

"Kind of a scary combination, isn't it?" Preston wiped some mustard from his chin.

"They are willing to hire you on a per diem basis. The Chief is certainly behind the idea, but I don't know how long the money is going to last."

"That's something, but I need to find a job that will pay some kind of benefits."

"I hear you. I wish I could help. Have you checked with the state troopers? They probably have more money to spare."

"Been there, done that. Everyone thinks it is important, but the bad guy you can see always gets priority over the bad guy you can't see. Besides, in order to get in the front door in police work, you have to have some kind of police training. Being a computer geek doesn't mean much to the people sorting résumés."

The crowd went wild as the home quarterback found an opening and tossed the ball long down the side. A perfect catch.

Ken Dixon leaned over to Preston and shouted over the roar, "I'll keep my eyes open for you."

Chapter 33

Ashley sat in the stony silence of the family dinner. Mother was at the table. She even looked kind of pretty. Her short hair had been curled, and a hint of blush gave her some much-needed color. Lisa must have helped her. Mother never did her hair anymore. At least not on her own.

Of course, Dad was useless on that front. Most fronts, really, Ashley thought. He always sat opposite her. Eating quietly. Meditating, she imagined, on some illustration he might use to bring greater illumination in his next sermon. Not that anyone would remember it anyway.

Ashley thought about her challenge. It was a pleasant distraction from the TV dinners. She could send a letter, maybe. Something short, sweet and very white. She thought for a while about this and ended up discarding the idea. Too elementary, not serious enough.

As usual, her dad finished supper with a reading. He opened the large family Bible and situated his half-frame reading glasses on his nose. He looked over the top of them at his family. Ashley wondered what the man was thinking. Was he really just going to read from the Bible and expect his wife to stop being a freak? Did he think that somehow this was a magic cure for her paranoia, the voices in her head, the horror that stalked their house at night, the lingering threat that she might just go completely off the deep end?

She stopped herself from sneering at him. She wanted to get up and leave. Walk away from the table and his empty religion. Even the sound of his voice irritated her. A voice people paid to come and listen to. That's how she saw it. Or, maybe all his congregants tolerated it like she did. Why, then, did they keep showing up? She guessed the idea that he was a reverend made them think that what he said was actually important or holy or something. They should try living with him, she thought. Better yet, they should ask Renee Hansel. Renee would probably have some stories to tell about her old man.

He thumbed through the onion skin pages to a spot that looked like it was somewhere near the end. He read the Bible like a manual—methodically and in perfect monotone. One part stuck out. "In the mouth of two or three witnesses shall every word be established."

Usually she remembered nothing. But that one verse seemed to be signaling to her.

Then it came to her, like a window opening up in her mind.

It will be just like hopscotch, Ashley decided. One box at a time.

Chapter 34

The weather was perfect. Just enough of a breeze to tease the edges of her skirt. The humidity dropped and the church filled with people. Ashley noticed a few new faces. Her father would be especially animated in his sermon. It always happened when the turnout was good.

Mrs. Hansel wore a white dress that wasn't exactly flirty, but it fit precisely. Battenberg lace over an inner polyester shell. Ashley wondered again if the woman wore it to impress her father. The thought made her feel cold inside. Ashley slipped into the pew next to the woman and sat down. Mrs. Hansel's husband didn't come to church. Ashley didn't know why.

The organist began playing, and the congregants stopped socializing and moved from the lobby into the serious zone of the sanctuary. Ashley started to imagine all the ways she could embarrass her father while he preached. If she concentrated hard enough, she could imagine away the sound of her father's voice. Almost. She dug her fingernails into her palms. Something to silence the hatred threatening to leak out.

Her dad finally finished his sermon and the organist followed with something bleak and tired-sounding. He walked somberly down the aisle with a pleasant, priestly smile on his face, so he could stand at the door and make everyone late for lunch. Ashley glanced at her reddened hands.

"What's the matter, honey?" Mrs. Hansel noticed her palms.

Ashley clamped her hands shut. "Nothing, I'm fine." The words came out before she could stop them. For a moment, Ashley wanted to believe the woman might really care, but for all she knew, Mrs. Hansel might be trying to worm her way into their family, effectively elbowing their mother out of the picture. Mother sat in the front row. She would never make it to church anymore if Lisa didn't help to get her ready. They came into the sanctuary early to "pray". No one interrupted their holy activity, and it kept questions to a minimum. It had worked so far.

"Really, dear. You can tell me if something is wrong." Mrs. Hansel sounded sincere enough, but she worked as a psychologist and was paid to sound sincere. Maybe it was an act.

Ashley saw her opening. "Can we talk somewhere?"

Mrs. Hansel seemed pleased and followed Ashley out through a side door and stopped above an infrequently used staircase going down to the basement. No one ever left the sanctuary this way.

Ashley crossed her arms to stop the shaking. Mrs. Hansel probably noticed. "Is something wrong, Ash?" Mrs. Hansel always called her Ash.

"I'm afraid, Mrs. Hansel, really afraid something bad is going to happen."

Mrs. Hansel put a hand on Ashley's shoulder. The affection felt kind, but Ashley pushed the thought away. She chewed her lip for a bit, staring at the floor. "Someone told me something, and I don't know what to do about it."

Renee waited for Ashley to continue.

"I heard about it in kind of a round-about way. Some boys at Florin are planning something."

"What do you mean?"

"You're a school board member there, right?" The woman nodded and Ashley continued. "There's a secret club, a white supremacist group, I guess."

"What are they planning, Ash?"

Chapter 35

"You're kidding right?" Chase Hikeman was not amused. "Where am I going to hide in there?"

"There's lots of places, Chase. Please. All I need is for you to find out what is really going on between them."

A wave of understanding passed over Chase's face. He pulled off his glasses, sat down on the cracked concrete stair outside his apartment block and began to clean the lenses. "I see." He rubbed them for a bit, then said, "Do you think they're having an affair?"

The sound of that from someone other than her sister made Ashley feel weird and tears began to sting her eyes. She looked away, but not before Chase noticed.

"I'm sorry. That wasn't sensitive of me." Chase pushed his glasses back onto his face and stood up. "I guess we better get going then. You'll cover for me if I get caught, right?"

Chapter 36

Philip Blithe pulled out breath freshener from the desk drawer and sprayed some into his mouth. The church vestry had been converted into an office. An ornate Persian rug covered the darkened chestnut flooring. The room contained a bookshelf, a desk and a pair of carved Louis XV armchairs recently reupholstered to match the rug. Philip checked his breath against his hand and put the spray away. He removed his collar, rolled it up carefully, and put it in the same drawer.

Renee Hansel knocked lightly on the door and came in. Right on time.

"Hi, Philip." She smiled at him.

He glanced quickly at her dress. "You look stunning. Please, make yourself comfortable."

Renee sat down.

"How's Bill?" Philip asked.

"He's doing great. We hope to take a little time off soon. He's been working crazy hours lately." Renee turned on her phone and touched the screen to pull up a list. "It looks like we've made quite a bit of progress on our holiday food drive. Mr. Mackery has offered to contact all the local grocers for donations and the ladies' group will take care of picking those up for us."

Philip rummaged through his desk and pulled out a notepad. "What have you heard about perishables?"

"I spoke with Fran about that. The Food Bank doesn't have refrigeration units, but Fran made arrangements with a butcher to rent space for the two weeks before Thanksgiving. We'll pick up our perishables during that time. Shouldn't be a problem."

"Is the Food Bank going to pack boxes for families, or do we need to manage that?" he asked.

"Fran said the local Lions Club is planning to help with that so we'll just need to have the food stuffs together before their work dates."

"Super." Phil double-checked his list before dropping it on his desk. "Thanks for taking care of all that."

Renee put her phone away and looked up at him. "How is she, Phil?"

Philip sank down in his chair. "Elizabeth?"

She nodded.

"Not good," he replied. "She's not sleeping well at night, but she seems to be in bed all day. When she gets up, she is either distant or irritable. I'm not sure which is worse."

"Is she taking her medication?"

"I can't be sure. She's often up fighting with whatever it is she fancies is after her. I've taken to sleeping in the office, you know."

"Why?"

"If she wakes up in a fit, she'll attack whoever is nearby."

Philip looked away from Renee. There were other pieces he didn't have to explain.

"I think the girls hate me."

"It's a hard time for all of you."

"They don't understand that if we put their mother into an institution, the church will run us out of here. They're nice folks, generally," he motioned vaguely toward the sanctuary beyond the closed door, "but they wouldn't tolerate a pastor with a wife in a mental institute, you know?

"If we left, the girls would lose their place at school. I don't want to do that to them in the middle of their high school years." Philip rubbed his face with both his hands. "We'll just have to manage somehow until they're done with school."

Renee shifted in her chair. "Look, I can't officially advise you because you're not on my case load, but you need to contact your psychiatrist and ask him to take another look at this."

Philip leaned forward on his elbows. "What else can he do?"

"What is she taking?"

"Trazodone and Quetiapine."

"Anything else?"

Philip shrugged. "Well, she's been taking oxycodone for lower back pain, but she's been taking that for years."

"Philip, if it were me, I'd call her psychiatrist and tell him that."

"Tell him what?"

"About the oxycodone. It can get pretty nasty if you mix it with the wrong stuff."

A glimmer of hope. He nodded. "I'll do that. Thanks, Renee."

"It's nothing." Renee waved away his thanks. "You know, there's something else I'd like to speak with you about."

"Please. Go ahead."

"It's a bit bizarre, but there seems to be some kind of white supremacist nonsense going on in the district. Ashley happened to mention that you have some new neighbors just a few doors down."

"Yes. We do. I confess I haven't gone to visit them yet, what with Elizabeth and all; I have fallen behind in my pastoral duties."

"I understand they are a black family."

"Yes, that is what I hear."

"I was just wondering if you could check in on them and tell them to let you know if they, or their son, have any problems. I think they might be more willing to speak to a pastor than a psychologist." She tucked her phone back into her handbag and tugged on the hem of her dress. "I plan to bring it up to the school superintendent at the next board meeting. I think it is something our community should be aware of."

"Certainly. Quite so." Philip stood when Renee did to see her out. "I'll make sure to check in on the family this week. I'll let you know if I hear anything."

Philip walked her to the office door and opened it. She turned and gave him a hug. "Hang in there, Philip."

"Thanks, Renee." Philip Blithe watched her walk down the aisle, out through the foyer. For a moment, the afternoon sun captured her in perfect silhouette before she was gone.

Chapter 37

Chase Hikeman waited until the Pastor left before climbing out of the choir loft. The carved spindles of the railing separating the choir from the rest of the church kept him well hidden while affording a perfect view of the door into the vestry.

He had only been hiding a few minutes when the woman came down the aisle. She must have gone somewhere for lunch after church, then come back. Chase decided she was beautiful, but she seemed serious and not guilty. He entertained some secret fantasies about listening to the juicy details of their 'meeting' but the central air conditioning came on, effectively erasing any sounds that might otherwise have made it through the rather large wooden door.

Chase soon lost interest in trying to listen and lost himself in the architecture of the church. It was constructed almost entirely of a beautiful grey stone and was one of the few places left in town with original scalloped, slate shingles on the roof. Lancet arches displayed lovely lead stained-glass windows wrapped in iron frames, and the carved door looked more like it belonged on some ancient cathedral. The church was, of course, not much larger than the houses in the area. He expected not more than two hundred people would be able to crowd together in the sanctuary. The intricacy of architectural detail extended even to the pews that reflected the lancet arches in the carvings on their sides.

Chase didn't believe in God, but the church was quiet and cooler than his apartment, and he decided it might not be such a bad place to hang out after all. Apart from the hum of the central air system, the place held a kind of stillness that never descended on his apartment.

Chase's attention snapped back to the present. The door opened and they appeared again. The lady smiled, reached out to give him a lingering hug, and invited him to call anytime.

Chase thought that didn't sound like such a bad idea. He flicked the thought away and watched her leave. The whole set up looked suspicious—a beautiful woman alone with a pastor in a place where no one was watching. It didn't look good, and Ashley was going to freak.

Chapter 38

"Don't lie to me, Chase." Ashley put her hands on her hips.

"Honest, I didn't hear anything. The air conditioners made too much white noise to make anything out."

"Are you sure you're not just trying to keep me from feeling bad?" Her face blanched.

She flung herself down on the torn brown sofa, the only furniture in Chase Hikeman's apartment. A Jack Russell jumped up beside her and nosed at her hand, wagging its pitiful stump of a tail.

"Get down, Finicky." The dog ignored Chase's command and curled up next to Ashley's legs.

Ashley stroked the dog, and Chase pretended not to be embarrassed by her tears.

"It could have been nothing, you know. They may just be good friends."

Ashley glowered at him, so he dropped it.

Chase just couldn't catch a break with this girl.

Chapter 39

Rosalyn Faraj picked up the local gazette which was delivered like some kind of drive-by shooting. She left the baking sidewalk and retreated into the cool of her kitchen. The boys were in the backyard, and she had no desire to join them. She didn't feel the need to throw around a ball that didn't roll, and she certainly didn't want to start sweating.

Several advertisements fell out of the center. She dropped these into the trash can in her kitchen.

The front page featured a feel-good story written about a fundraiser sponsored by a family in memory of their daughter whom they lost to cancer.

Rosalyn skimmed the article and turned the page.

Moving to this area was a huge adjustment. People were polite, generally, but not friendly. At least not the kind of friendly that could lead to friendship. She supposed most folks found relationships in their churches, but the Faraj family didn't go to church, and they decided not to try to pursue involvement with a mosque yet. They needed time to settle in, figure out their new schedules, get Jared adjusted to school.

Her finger stopped cold over an article in the bottom right hand corner of page two. She picked it up and read. Her fingers trembled just a bit.

The back patio door slid open. Rosalyn folded the paper and dropped it in the trash just before they entered the kitchen.

Chapter 40

DIGA logged in less than 12 hours after his last session. His stomach churned, and his mouth was dry.

He waited for The Moderator to come online.

Change your mind, DIGA?

DIGA didn't respond directly. He wanted to lash out. He wanted to hurt The Moderator. Instead he reached for the bottle next to him, turned it on its end and took a large swallow. Then he typed, *What are my options?*

You have two.

Two?

Option A: You make her attempt suicide.

Or? DIGA's fought with his fingers to hold down the keys to make the question mark.

Option B: I tell the world that you are gay.

Chapter 41

Ashley hit the print button for what she hoped was the last time that night. Her eyes burned from staring at the screen. It had been quite an education after all.

She slid the papers into pocket protectors, rolled them together and slid them carefully down in the side of her backpack next to an old sheet. As it turned out, there really was a white supremacist group just one county over. They didn't even try to hide. Their website helped her get some ideas together and refine her rhetoric.

Ashley threw the pack over her shoulder and crept down the stairs with her shoes off before sneaking out the side door by the kitchen that led into the garage. She turned on her flashlight and followed the shelf past the rusting tins of mineral spirits and peeling paint trays. Then she found it. One can of yellow spray paint. She picked up and heard the mixing ball roll slowly.

"Yes," she whispered. It wasn't empty. Ashley hoped for red, but yellow would do.

The night air felt great and she walked along the sidewalk instead of following the creek all the way through town. She figured if someone saw her on the sidewalk, they wouldn't think anything of it. Besides there were way too many spiders down by the creek path and she didn't care to have any creature legging his way over her neck at this time of night.

She glanced at her watch. Going in would be easy. Getting out would be another problem altogether. The later it got, the more suspicious people would become. Ashley reached the old sycamore tree in the park right around 10 p.m.

"Post meridiem." Ashley tongued the Latin words, imitating her eccentric professor. She continued past the house Chase and she had explored and slipped into the woods. She could hear the mosquitoes and knew waiting would only result in a blood-letting.

Ashley made a run for the doorway they used on their first trip into the underground chamber. No lights illuminated the basement. She felt her way past the hand-hewn pillars into the attached carriage house and pulled open the low green door. The loud scraping sound as the door dragged over the gravel floor was louder than she remembered. Something moved nearby, and she shoved herself through the door way before it opened entirely. She sat there panting. Waiting. Listening. Pressing the flashlight against her chest to keep it dark.

Nothing. She chanced a shaft of light back toward the opening where she entered. An old tabby cat stood staring at her, its eyes glowing an unearthly green.

Ashley's heart pounded. She hadn't expected it to feel as creepy in here without Chase.

Now she just wanted to get it over with. She sat in what was once a cold cellar, but the cellar also contained a hidden entrance to a chamber with another purpose entirely. She pulled back on a piece of plywood beside her and stared at the opening in the brick. The blackness beyond swallowed her light, but she pressed on. Crouching over, she slid one leg carefully through the opening. Her backpack caught on the bricks, and she twisted her arms out of it as she maneuvered herself all the way through the opening. Then she reached back for her pack and turned to face the hidden hallway.

The dressed stone walls rose in a gentle arch overhead just low enough for her to reach up and pick off the tiny crumbling stalactites that had formed over the last two hundred years or so. They looked like bits of snot hanging from the arched cobblestone ceiling. The damp air lay cold and breathless over the muddy floor, pock-marked by drops of water that dripped relentlessly off the tips of the stalactites.

Ashley pushed back the panic of the dark, close place and followed the vague footprints in the mud from her last visit here with Chase. The hallway snaked almost 30 feet away from the cold cellar before turning and opening into a chamber. The room itself was almost 15 feet wide and about 25 feet long.

At one end, what may have been a chimney hole—now filled in with earth and rock—rose over the roof. An antique tin of lamp oil sat rusting away in the corner. Beyond this, there were no other indications that anyone else came here.

No wonder, Ashley thought. It was perpetually damp and cold and dark.

"A perfect place for a crime." She allowed herself a moment to imagine what unfettered hatred could accomplish in a place with no windows to the outside world, where no one could hear the victim's scream. She heard stories like this, of course. Until Chase had brought her down here, she never imagined that such a place could really exist in her own no-account town in southern Pennsylvania.

Gooseflesh rose on her arms. Cutis anserine, she thought. Goosebumps. Her Latin teacher was always trying to connect the dead language to the real world.

"Cutis anserina." Ashley turned off her flashlight and spoke the words aloud into the chamber. The mud-covered floor and cold stone seemed to swallow her voice so completely it sounded as if someone else far away spoke the words.

Time to get busy, Ashley turned on her light again and unzipped her pack.

Chapter 42

DIGA sat down on the edge of his bed and pulled out a single, unlined sheet of paper. Taking a compass from his backpack, he drew a circle near the center of the paper just large enough to hold the short message. He took the crayons in his left hand and began to write. Instead of looking childish, it looked artsy, like a cute birthday card greeting.

He placed the writing near the center, keeping the page evenly balanced.

The words '*You'll make the world a better place*' hung across the top half of the circle.

He slid the note in a folder and slipped it into his gym bag behind the roll of his towel. DIGA waited for the sound of the garage door opening as his dad left for work. Then he walked down the stairs to the kitchen. As usual, his mother wasn't up. She didn't believe in mornings.

DIGA grabbed a tall glass of orange juice and a bagel. He downed the juice quickly, stuffed the bagel in his pocket and went out. The garage always had that unusual smell. Grease and old car fumes and something else he couldn't name. He lifted his bike from the rack on the wall and maneuvered it out through the side door. The team met at 8 a.m. for early swim conditioning.

He could have borrowed his mom's car, but he always preferred riding. He hated having to ask his mom for anything.

Chapter 43

Pastor Philip Blithe stared at himself in the hallway mirror and removed the clerical collar. He undid the buttons on his dark blue shirt and let the collar relax. The girls had already gone off to school, and Elizabeth was sleeping, he hoped. It seemed she was almost always sleeping now.

Sometimes it didn't seem so long ago that he would walk back across the lawn over lunch and find her singing in the kitchen or talking to the flowers she worked in all around the rectory. He would pat her playfully on the bottom, and they would sit down together like a couple of newlyweds to talk about their day.

Philip sighed. It seemed like another life, and sometimes that other life threatened to eat him alive. Suddenly he was living with a woman he didn't know. Romance vanished. Disappointment gnawed away at his sleep. It was easy enough for him to share the kindness of God with his parishioners. He let out a sarcastic grunt. His own God didn't seem to care.

In fact, he had all but stopped praying for his wife. Praying just made him long for change. It was easier to go numb and stop hoping and try to forget what he wanted.

He changed his mind and put the collar back on. It would make the introduction simpler. He wouldn't have to prove he wasn't selling something. He refastened his collar buttons and walked out of the house. It had rained overnight. The street was wet, and water still dripped from the trees overhead.

Instead of heading to the rectory, Pastor Blithe walked down the sidewalk to the end of the block and turned right. In a couple of minutes he stood in front of an old brownstone house with a large porch. It was a lovely house. The corner turrets even boasted rounded glass in rounded sashes. He pinched at his collar and walked up the stone stairs onto the porch. He noticed the flowers freshly planted in the beds alongside the porch and was reminded of Elizabeth.

Philip reached up to knock just as the door pulled open. A black woman startled at the sight of someone on her porch and almost dropped her watering can.

"I'm sorry." Philip took a half step back. "I was just about to ring the bell. I'm Pastor Philip Blithe. I think you might have already met my daughter?"

The woman's face relaxed into a smile. "Lovely girl, yes. I'm Rosalyn Faraj." She pinned the watering can against her chest, so she could shake his hand.

"I just wanted to stop in and make my acquaintance. Is this a bad time for you?"

"Not at all. Do you mind if I water the flowers while we talk? I've mixed up some plant food for them. It's my feeble attempt at recreating paradise."

"Of course."

"So, you're Ashley's dad?" Rosalyn walked down the stairs. Pastor Blithe leaned against one of the porch railings and wished he had left the clerical collar at home.

"Yes, I actually have two girls. Lisa is Ashley's older sister. She's seventeen already." The memory of what used to be threatened to break in again on his present, but he pushed past it. "Do you have children?"

"Yes, my son is seventeen. He's joined the second week of football camp over at Florin High. Their coach must be determined to keep the grocers in business."

"Why is that?"

"If all those boys come home as hungry as my Jared, their parents are going to have to start working overtime to keep up with the food bills."

Philip chuckled and relaxed. He sat down on the top step and waited for Mrs. Faraj to finish.

"I'm sorry, I should have offered you a chair."

"No, this is fine."

"Easy for you to say. If anyone sees a pastor sitting on my porch stairs, they just might take exception to my hospitality." She meant it as a joke, but there was an edge in her voice.

"I'm sure no one will mind." Pastor Blithe squinted up at the blue sky beyond the porch roof. "I did want to check in with you, though."

"Check in, how?" Rosalyn set the empty watering can down on the bottom step and looked up at the pastor.

"See how school is going for Jared and how you're settling in. Invite you to services, if you're looking for a church—" Philip cut himself off. He suddenly remembered they were Moslems.

"Thank you. I'm not quite sure how to answer that question." Rosalyn looked up the empty street. "I have heard things that give me some concern."

"Is that so?"

"Did you read the article in the gazette that appears on our sidewalks?"

"Which one?"

"The one mentioning a white supremacist group recruiting kids from the high school."

Philip hadn't noticed the article. "No, I didn't see that. Has your son been having trouble at the school?"

"Not per se. Since I read that article, I've found myself filtering everything Jared tells me about his day, his coach, his peers." She looked hard at the pastor. "Is my son safe here?"

Pastor Blithe didn't know how to answer. He only just heard about the news from Renee Hansel. "I hope so, Mrs. Faraj."

"You *hope* so? What does that mean?"

"I heard about the situation from a friend who happens to work at Florin High. She's a school psychologist. She asked me to check in and see if your son was having any trouble because of all this."

Chapter 44

A whistle sounded and nine athletes plunged into the water from starting blocks. They remained under for a few seconds before surfacing and breaking into the butterfly stroke. Three of the swimmers gained an early lead. Coach Drew walked along side. He shouted encouragement here and there, but mostly he just studied their form, making mental notes.

The three completed their flip turns at almost exactly the same time, pushing off hard from the wall to finish the next 50 meter laps. They emerged again, this time in free stroke.

The coach followed them back to the start and touched his timer when the first of the three reached the end of the pool. He studied the stopwatch in disbelief.

Coach Drew waited until all nine finished the drill. "Get out. Dry off. Line up."

The swimmers breathed a sigh of relief and pulled themselves from the water. Coach Drew didn't believe in off-season for swimmers and ran unofficial training year-round for five members of his swim team at the local YMCA pool.

Most of the varsity swim team comprised juniors and seniors who joined the program in their elementary years. The swim team wasn't celebrated like high school football, but in competitive swimming circles, Coach Drew's team was a force to be reckoned with.

The boys all lined up beside the pool for a quick meeting. The coach clapped three times and the team responded with five claps in perfect unison.

"Gentlemen. Nice work today. You keep that up, and you'll go places. Quinn, get your head into water just a bit before your hands on the butterfly. Jake, nice work on that turn in the shallows."

The boys chuckled. Jake was the tallest competitive swimmer the school had seen and the coach thought for sure he would crack his head on the bottom of the pool.

"Firth. Garbold. Anderson. Come see me. The rest of you to the showers. I'll see you tomorrow. Bright and early."

The three boys gathered around their coach as the others headed to the locker room. Coach Drew folded his arms across his chest and waited until the others were out of earshot. "I've been watching my clock today, boys."

Darren Firth shot a glance at the other two and spoke up. "Coach, we were going as fast as we could."

"I don't think so." The swimmers drooped. No one wanted to disappoint the coach.

"Nope. I don't think so." A smile played at the corner of Coach Drew's mouth. "But you *were* swimming faster than I've ever seen."

The boys looked up, surprised. Coach drew clapped Darren on his shoulder. "Captain, I think your team might have a chance at nationals." He walked off, leaving the three standing in shock.

Anderson punched the air in celebration and the muscles on his chest stood to attention.

Darren turned to his team mates. "Men, we're not just going to nationals; we're going to rock nationals!"

After some chest thumping, the three headed to the locker room.

#

Darren stood on the bench that ran between the lockers and whistled to get his team's attention. His towel tight around his middle. "Team, the coach just said you're too slow for states—"

The team erupted in complaints and denials, but Darren raised his hand and waited for the team to get quiet before adding, "but he thinks you might be fast enough for nationals."

The team members all found a locker and started their own thunder roll. Darren laughed and waited for them to quiet down again. "But it isn't going to happen if we don't work our butts off. By the beginning of the season, we'll need to be butt-less and very fast."

They laughed at the joke, and he raised his hand again. "Hey, before you leave, would you guys mind signing a card for my kid cousin? He's having a tough time, and he's kind of a swimming nut. Just sign around the circle in the middle of the card. He'd like that."

They swarmed the paper he set out and fought over the pen until they all signed their names to it.

Then Darren slipped the paper back into its folder and put it away.

Chapter 45

Dr. Adam Faraj arrived on the last train and disembarked onto the wooden platform that made up Florin's attempt at a train station. The silver Amtrak passenger cars pulled away leaving the tired doctor standing in the humid evening at the base of a gully. A single light burned from atop its post.

The rail line cut deep through the town to allow traffic to flow unencumbered overhead. The passenger platform sat well below grade, and the few travelers who hopped the train here used a wooden stairway that dropped down from a parking lot above.

A set of LED lights installed on the stairs cast a cold blue light across the treated lumber. Adam bent down to fix a shoe lace and then shouldered the strap of his attaché case and walked to the stairs.

He reached for the handrail at the bottom but stopped and squinted in the evening gloom at the risers between the stair treads. He hadn't noticed it that morning, but then he wouldn't have been able to see it on his way down. Someone had drawn something on the risers. Adam took several steps back and looked at it again. Starting at the bottom riser was a caricature of a person in a white robe wearing a tall pointed hat. In the LED light it seemed to glow with a kind of surreal blue. The eye holes were left blank, but the graffiti extended over the risers of a full seven stairs.

Adam walked forward and ascended slowly, studying the drawing. Above the drawing, awkward chalk letters scrawled a message across the remaining stairs. *Leave. Before. You. Get. Hurt.*

"Adam." Adam looked up. Rosalyn stood at the top of the platform, looking down at him. She wore a simple orange maxi dress. Adam had forgotten their dinner plans.

"Hello beautiful." He climbed the rest of the stairs. The risers toward the top were blank. Apparently whoever wrote the message didn't want to be seen by anyone who happened to be in the parking lot.

"Everything okay?" Rosalyn noticed her husband was distracted by something other than his favorite dress.

"No. Everything's fine. Just tired." He knew she wouldn't be able to see the graffiti from her vantage point.

She put one hand on her hip and looked coyly at him. "You still up for our date?"

He kissed her when he reached the top stair. "Of course. Wouldn't miss it." He breathed in the scent of her perfume.

"Where are you taking me?" she asked.

"I've heard there is a quiet restaurant on the other side of town where we might find a hot meal and a dark corner." He gave her a pat as they turned to the car.

"Lead me on," she said.

"What is Jared doing?" he asked.

"Sleeping in front of the television." She chuckled. "The young man has no energy left after practice."

Chapter 46

Ashley found Jasmín coming out of chemistry. She grabbed her by the hand and led her out onto the flagstone patio where the girls often ate lunch. The flags, as it was known, were empty and Ashley picked an iron picnic table shaded by an umbrella.

Jasmín seemed to have gotten over her suspicions about Ashley and the online game. Jasmín had apologized for her comments, and the two became even closer. Jasmín regularly asked about Ashley's mom. Jasmín was the twin sister she never had.

"What's going on?" Jasmín asked. "Something wrong?"

"Everything." Ashley felt her face blush with shame.

"What's the matter? Is your mom okay?"

"Jazz. I just don't know what to do." Tears ran down her cheeks again. They made dark mascara smudges beneath her eyes.

Jasmín reached into her backpack and handed Ashley a tissue.

"You want to talk about it," Jasmín put her hand on Ashley's arm, "or do you want to get drunk?"

Ashley laughed, in spite of herself. Jasmín could always seem to make her laugh.

"I don't know. I've never tried it."

"You should. It's the most fun you'll never remember." The two laughed again and Ashley cleaned up the smears under her eyes with the help of a compact.

"It's my dad," Ashley whispered. "I think he's having an affair."

"No shit."

"I know, right?" Ashley blew her nose and tossed the tissue onto the table. She could feel the same old hatred boiling up inside her. It didn't help that the other woman was beautiful and kind and friendly and everything her own mother had been before she got sick.

"How do you know?" Jasmín whispered back the question.

"Well, I don't *know* exactly. A friend hid in the choir loft when dad and the woman were in a 'counseling' appointment." He saw them hugging before she left.

"Your dad is a counselor?"

"Well, not exactly. Well, he never tells us if it is for counseling or church business. For some reason people think ministers have some kind of direct line to God, or something."

"And he counsels women?"

"Yes."

"Alone?" Jasmín was incredulous. "That's crazy. And you think he's getting something for his time?"

Ashley's face grew blotchy. "I don't know what to do, Jasmín."

"Do? What you need to do is catch him at it."

"Catch him? Like how?"

"Hello, nanny-cam."

"What's that?"

"Gretchen got one from her boyfriend, although she didn't know what it was until much later."

Ashley grimaced. "You mean he was spying on her?"

"Yes, but he was a freak."

"What does it look like?"

"I think the best ones are hidden in clocks. Some are motion-activated and have audio and video recording which is saved onto a memory card. He'll never guess." Jasmín pulled up an Internet browser on her phone and thumbed in the search string. She handed the phone to Ashley.

"This is $85!" Ashley groaned.

"Well, how much is your parent's marriage worth to you?" Jasmín pushed. She knew Ashley didn't walk around with the kind of spending money most of the other girls at Sutherland Hall seemed to have.

"What would I do with the disk when I got it?"

"Give it to me and then tell him you have it." Jasmín asked.

"Why?"

"You wouldn't want him to find it, would you?"

Ashley slumped back into her chair, thinking about how to find the money for it. Jasmín seemed to be reading her mind.

"I'll tell you what. I want to buy it for you. Consider it an early birthday present. Maybe you can catch the creep in the act."

"Jasmín, that's just gross." Ashley leaned forward and put her face in her hands.

Chapter 47

A police secretary buzzed Preston Farwick through the security door into the office.

"Good morning, Mr. Farwick. Chief Gregson is expecting you. Can I get you some coffee?"

"Yes. Thanks." She pushed back on her office chair, and he followed her into the officer's lounge. She poured a cup of coffee into a blue mug with a gold "50" across the side.

"Someone turn 50?" Farwick asked.

"No. Last year marked the anniversary of our department."

"I see."

"Cream and sugar?"

"Please. Two creams, two sugars. Got to keep the bubble in the middle." Farwick patted his stomach.

The secretary chuckled and handed him the mug. "Follow me, I'll show you in."

The police department office suite held all the warmth of a doctor's office. A few plastic ferns had been placed in strategic places to soften the atmosphere. Even so, it took a while for folks to get over the awkwardness of trying to communicate through security glass before being allowed in.

She stopped in front of a door labeled with "Chief Gregson" in black vinyl letters. She knocked once and opened the door. "Hey, Chief, Mr. Farwick is here to see you."

She motioned for him to enter.

The chief got up from his chair. "Mr. Farwick. Thanks for coming in. Ken Dixon has quite a lot to say about you."

"Oh, boy. What did he say exactly?"

"Mostly that you're the guy we need around here to keep our kids safe."

Preston Farwick gave half a smile. "It's a crazy world when a police department needs to hire a computer geek. Sure isn't what it used to be like when we were kids, you know?"

"Ain't that the truth." Gregson lifted a folder from a black wire basket on his desk. "We get calls from parents every week about their kids doing stuff online or on their cell phones that they don't understand. Of course, some of those are the same parents who keep calling. The best we can do is tell them to warn their kids about the danger and keep their eyes on what the kids are up to. Problem is, most parents don't know how to do it, and the ones that do have kids that know how to get around the parental controls." Gregson looked up from the folder. "You have any kids?"

Preston Farwick took a quick sip of coffee. "No. Wife couldn't, you know."

Gregson grimaced at himself for asking the question. "Sorry to hear that."

"It's okay; we have a dog. She count?" Preston smiled.

"My dog sure thinks so. Damn creature thinks she owns the furniture."
He pulled a post-it note from his desk, stuck it onto the first page of the
folder and wrote something on it. "What I'd really like to do, Mr.
Farwick, is to offer you a full-time position."

"That's what my wife would like you to do, too," Preston said.

"I hear you. I'm hoping that with luck and some hard work on your part,
we can convince the board that our children would be a lot safer if you
were full time here."

"What are the odds of that?" Preston asked.

"Not good. The board members aren't exactly connected to the world
these kids are living in, you know? They're not bad folks, just out of
touch. I think they can be persuaded; I only hope nothing bad has to
happen before they see the need for someone like you working as part of
our team." Gregson handed the folder to Farwick. "This includes the
transcripts from a bunch of cell phones we confiscated. Nothing much
we could do with them, except download the copy and give 'em back. Of
course, we slapped a few kids on the hands for having skimpy pictures of
their girlfriends. Most kids nowadays don't realize they could be charged
if she's under the age of 18." Gregson gestured at the folder. "What I'm
looking for are leads on something more sinister than the hormonal
activity of a bunch of minors with camera phones."

"What do you suspect?" Preston Farwick set his mug down and flipped
open the folder.

"Some kind of outside player," Gregson replied.

Farwick glanced quickly through the papers, taking in more than the
casual observer. "These kids aren't stupid, just—" he stopped and

glanced around as if looking for the word, "naïve. They don't realize the stakes involved. Kids caught by stalkers usually end up dead."

"Funny that."

"What?"

"Kids aren't stupid, just naïve. Their parents *are* stupid, at least when it comes to the Internet—"

"But not naïve," Farwick finished the thought.

"Right. The people operating the equipment don't have the maturity to use it. Those who do have the maturity, don't know how it operates. It's a bad combination."

"What do you want me to do with this?" Preston Farwick tested the weight of the manila folder in his free hand.

"Work a miracle." Chief Gregson wasn't smiling. "If you can pull that off, I can almost guarantee you'll be looking at a full-time job."

"I'll see what I can do."

"Super." Chief Gregson pulled another folder from his pile and checked inside to make sure it was the one he wanted. "We'll need you to get a child-abuse clearance, and complete a criminal background check as soon as you can. Every employee or subcontractor has to have those on file in our office. Until then, we'll have to pretend you aren't really working here."

Chapter 48

Rosalyn sat cross-legged on the cushioned porch swing. Adam stood next to the screen door staring up at the sky. Thunder rolled dark and heavy through the humid air. He inhaled the scent of rain.

"It looks like it is going to be a cracker of a storm."

"Adam, I'm serious. Jared hasn't said anything to me about it, but he has to have been hearing things at school."

"You can't just assume the reason his coach hasn't played him is because he's black."

"You know as well as I do that he is probably the best player on that team. His last coach almost had a coronary when we told him we were moving out here."

Adam turned and leaned against the porch post to face his wife. "I know, but just about every coach won't play a kid who hasn't served his time in training. Besides, I've met the man. Seems like a decent sort."

"The world is full of decent people who don't like black men." Rosalyn was upset with her husband's ambivalence. "Adam. I'm not interested in my son growing up in a place where he isn't going to get a fair shake just because of the color of his skin."

"Let's not forget why we moved out here. Jared needs to experience something other than big city life." He sat down next his wife and pulled her close.

"I know, I remember. It isn't like we're the only black people in the area. I just expected it to feel different out here."

"We need to give it more time, find a place to plug into the community."

"You mean like a church?" Rosalyn looked up at his face.

Adam laughed softly. "Yeah, like a church."

"The pastor came to visit me yesterday," Rosalyn said.

"Was he nice?"

"He was distant. Reserved."

"Reserved?"

"Adam, I think he came to warn us."

"Warn us about what?"

"Haven't you been listening to me?" Rosalyn got up from the swing and crossed her arms. "There are people around here that don't like black folks. And they just might be the kind of people who aim to do something about what they don't like. There's even a group in the local school."

"What kind of a group?"

Rosalyn pulled the clipping of the article from her pocket and handed it to him.

Adam pulled out his phone and turned on the flashlight app so he could read it.

Rosalyn waited without speaking until he was finished. He folded the paper and handed it back to her. "Has Jared seen this?" he asked.

"I don't think so."

"Good, come here." He took his wife's hand and pulled her down onto his lap. "Listen. This is a scary time, but I have a good feeling about this. People just need to get to know us a bit. I think it is all going to work out."

She looked directly into his face. "Dr. Faraj. That is exactly what you say when you have to tell one of your patients they have Stage 4 cancer."

Chapter 49

DIGA sat cross-legged on the floor of his bedroom. He didn't really care if anyone found him crying. He would just tell them another lie. Besides, there was little chance his parents would get home before he left again. DIGA picked up the crayon and finished underneath the first line. He sat up and backhanded the tears from his face. The script was perfectly elementary in its style.

You'll make the world a better place,

when you leave it.

Signatures surrounded the circle. The swim team had all signed it. Every one of them. Now he was going to betray them as well.

Chapter 50

Preston Farwick handed his papers to the clerk in the UPS store. She motioned toward a young black man seated next to a live scan machine. He walked over and handed him the paperwork. The young man wiped the face of the glass scanner which was about the size of an index card.

"You do a lot of these?" Farwick asked.

"Depends. Goes in spurts." He took Farwick's fingers one by one and rolled them onto the glass. As he did, Farwick's digital fingerprint showed up on the monitor in front of the clerk.

"So much for black ink and special cards, eh?"

"Yep. The live scan machine uploads the images to the FBI database, where they're checked against existing records."

"I imagine some people get kinda nervous about this."

"Some do. I guess most of the bad guys find a line of work where their employer doesn't require prints." The clerk wiped down the screen before moving onto Farwick's thumb. "The fidgety ones I see are those who think the government is out to get them."

Farwick chuckled at the thought and watched as the print lines of his last finger appeared in black on the screen.

"You're all done." The clerk clicked the submit button on the monitor and wiped down the scan glass. "You'll get the clearance form in the mail in about a week."

"That fast?"

The clerk smiled. "Not bad for the government."

Chapter 51

Lisa Blithe situated herself in the chair next to her mother's bed. The woman slept, peaceful now. It seemed the only peace the woman ever got was when she finally went to sleep, and that only came after she took her meds.

Elizabeth Blithe couldn't swallow whole pills anymore. Somehow in her mind, the pills threatened to choke her. Lisa had taken to crushing the tiny pink pills in a spoon like her mother did for her when she was a toddler. Lisa would stir in applesauce or yogurt to mask the foul taste. Her mother would open her mouth like a baby bird and swallow the medicine.

"Thank you, Lisa." It was one of the few times her mother seemed to recognize her or speak kindly to her.

Lisa looked at the woman in the bed. "They never stop, Lisa." Her mother said, "They just never stop." Lisa wanted it to be over. Lisa could almost hear the voices her mother complained about. The fear around the woman seemed to creep out from her and play games on Lisa's skin.

She wanted the voices to stop. She wanted her mother to get better. She wanted to stop being afraid. Afraid of her own voices. Afraid that she would end up like her mother. Wasted. Empty. Terrified.

Lisa shuffled through the mail in her lap and found another of the ugly letters. They had become more and more frequent. Lisa knew she should just throw them away. But then she would hear her own voice whispering. Let the ugly out. Let it out.

In one part of her brain, Lisa could sit beside herself and make sense of the craziness. She told herself she was acting like an addict. Like someone who just has to have one more fix.

You think you have control over this, but you don't, Lisa. You can't control it.

And yet Lisa would open the letter.

She would always open the letters.

Chapter 52

Preston Farwick sat at the temporary work area they had given him in the police station. Since he began, it seemed as if worried parents materialized out of nowhere asking the police to scrutinize their kids' communications. Farwick downloaded and printed the transcripts. The files lay open in front him. He separated the transcripts into piles arranged according to a common thread. His mind worked through the contents of each cell phone transcript like a master chess player intent on determining his opponent's next move.

"Any luck?" Ken Dixon poked his head around the edge of the office cubicle. "You look pretty intent."

"Not much. Some of this is just the usual kid nonsense. Some isn't."

"What do you mean?"

"Online stalkers are like poker players. They do their best to determine what cards the other players are holding."

"Cards?"

"Online a person's 'cards' are his or her identity. The reason kids get into trouble is because they think they can be anonymous. Anonymity gives them license to do what they would never do face to face."

"So how does a stalker figure out who he is targeting?"

"Sometimes he'll trick them into giving a tell."

"Tells, like in poker?"

"Yes. When one player 'gives away' what he's holding or what he is planning on doing."

"Surely kids know better than to give out personal information." Ken Dixon pulled up a free chair and sat down next to the desk with Farwick's neat piles.

"No. More often an online stalker finds out something else about them that leads him to their real identity."

"How do you stop him?"

"If I'm lucky and very clever, I might be able to identify the tells of the person they are talking to online." Preston Farwick shuffled through the papers to find what he was looking for. "Just like them, my goal is to find some kind of identifying information."

"Like an address?"

Preston Farwick looked at his friend to find out if the question was serious. He realized Ken wasn't joking. "No. Stalkers would never leave their email address or an IP address floating around. Never. They are much smarter than that." He turned back to his piles. "First, I need to rule out what I think is just aimless chatter. I separate these out and look at the others for patterns."

"Have you found anything?"

"Maybe. It is too early to tell. These 13 kids made contact with someone online they don't know. Based on the context, I can assume they didn't know this person ahead of time. See? That's a tell. Having isolated these, I look closer for other patterns. Take a look." Preston pulled out three transcripts tagged with blue flags.

Ken Dixon studied the narrative. Nothing much. "Looks like they're playing some kind of game. Seems innocent enough."

"Maybe. Hard to tell. Anything else stand out to you?" Farwick asked.

"Not really."

"Look at this." Preston reached for a highlighter and marked the incoming and outgoing time stamp on each transmission. It took a couple of minutes. "See it now?"

"Sorry. I feel like I'm looking at one of those dot pictures, but I just can't make it out."

Preston grew animated. "That's because you are looking at what you can see."

"Help me." Dixon threw up his hands.

"Look at what is between what you can see."

"Sorry, Preston, I'm just not getting it."

Preston laughed, enjoying his friend's frustration. "Two minutes."

"Two minutes, 'til what? Two minutes until you tell me the answer?"

"No. These three kids are all online with someone who always waits exactly two minutes before responding. Look again."

Ken Dixon bent over the page and followed the highlighted sections. "Is that supposed to mean something?"

"It's the same for every single one of this guy's initial transmissions. It is his tell. Let's take a look at the stats. These three kids each logged over five conversations with this guy. Every single time he made them wait exactly two minutes before he responded to their first message. The odds that three people meet a 'new' person online who happens to have exactly the same time signature is extremely rare." Preston Farwick saw the light start to come on in his friend's mind. "It means these three kids have a common enemy."

"Is this enough to take to the chief?"

"It's compelling, but it isn't conclusive."

"Why would the guy wait two minutes? What purpose would it serve?"

"It's a tease; it builds suspense." Preston put the papers back on the correct pile. "It also tells us something about this guy. He is probably from this area. He wants high levels of control. Guys who want lots of control usually have an agenda."

Dixon grimaced. "And it probably isn't a good one." Ken Dixon lowered his voice and nodded toward the chief's office. "What did he tell you?"

"Pretty much what you said he'd say. We need you. We can't give you full-time hours. Hopefully horrible never happens, but when it does, you'll probably have a job."

"Makes sense."

"Yeah, not really. Let's let the kids get hurt first, then we'll hire you. So much for 'serve and protect,' eh?"

Chapter 53

Chase Hikeman and Ashley Blithe huddled under the pavilion at the park and waited for it to stop pouring. Ashley sat on the picnic table hugging her knees. She pulled her blonde hair back into a simple pony tail to keep it off her neck. She dressed in such a way that many thought she was older than fifteen. Chase Hikeman still hadn't begun to grow. In fact, he had pretty much given up on that ever happening.

Rain sluiced off the pavilion's roof, forming rivulets around the edge.

"Are you still feeling sad?" Chase wasn't afraid to ask direct questions.

He felt his breath catch for a moment as she looked him in the eyes.

"I'm going to catch him, Chase." She turned and stared out at the park streaming with water.

"What do you mean?"

"I'm going to record his next 'counseling' session." She clenched her jaw, grinding away at the anger.

"You sure that's a good idea? I don't really think that's legal."

Ashley glared at him.

Chase backed down. "Forget it."

"You want to help?"

"No."

"Come on, Chase."

"Nope."

"How about for a kiss?"

He looked over at her, his resolve shifting. "Maybe." He jumped down from the table opposite her. "What am I saying? I'd love to kiss you," he kicked at a stone, "but I don't want to have to pay for it. That's just gross. My mom does that sometimes—" he broke off and turned away from her.

"I'm sorry. I didn't mean it like that," she said.

"Yeah, sure."

"Never mind. I'll take care of it."

Chapter 54

Water dripped through the cobblestone on the ceiling of the underground chamber. Each droplet paused briefly on the bulbous tip of tiny tubular stalactites. The dissolved limestone from the soil above added infinitesimal amounts to the mineral deposits.

The drips from above and rising groundwater conspired to erase Ashley's footsteps from the floor of the catacomb.

Chapter 55

Ashley Blithe stopped into the church on her way home from school. She felt like she was being swallowed in the silence. It gave her the creeps. The air inside the sanctuary felt cooler even though her dad turned off the building's air conditioning during the week.

She walked quickly to the vestry office. She pressed her ear against the door. Nothing. She wasn't allowed in there. Now that she was about to enter, she wasn't certain what she might find.

Behind her yawned an empty sanctuary. For a fleeting instant, the faces of those who came for Sunday services watched her, scrutinized her, judged her.

She decided she hated them, too.

The iron door knob was cold in her hand. Ashley gave it a turn and pushed her way into the inner sanctum of her father's inviolate world. Gently she closed the door behind her. She stared down at the original wide-plank chestnut flooring. Bookshelves lined the wall. A single legal pad sat in the middle of the desk covered in her father's flowing handwriting. Sermon notes. The room looked much like his office over in the rectory. It even smelled like him. Two upholstered chairs sat to one side of his desk, a chaise lounge on the other.

In the other corner, a schefflera sat soaking in a glittering shaft of sunlight pouring from the single window in the vestry wall.

It seemed almost magical. Ashley stood mesmerized by the beauty of it. The stained glass transformed sunlight into a kaleidoscope of color. She walked toward it and reached out her hand, forgetting why she had come.

Her palm filled with a sunrise-pink that spilled out between her fingers and dripped down on the variegated foliage underneath.

"Beautiful, isn't it?" The voice came from right behind her.

Ashley spun around. "Daddy!"

"Sorry to startle you. I was over at the house and saw you stop in here. I figured you might be looking for me."

Ashley's mind scrambled to find words. "Yes. I thought you might be here." A cloud passed over the sun outside. The magic around the leaves of the schefflera disappeared. "I have something for you." She reached into her bag and pulled out the digital clock. Ashley walked over and set it on one of the shelves. Before she turned around, she twisted open the side of the clock camera and turned the switch on. "Someone gave it to me. It doesn't exactly match, but I thought you could use it."

Her father looked surprised and fumbled for words. She walked toward the door and gave him a wave before pulling the door shut behind her.

Chapter 56

Jasmín thumbed in her password. She wound one of the longer curls round and around her finger while she waited. Ashley seemed to have no idea that Jasmín was collecting everything for The Moderator. It had all been pathetically simple.

Jasmín looked up at the bulletin board hanging in her room. A picture of the two of them stared back. That photo booth ate five whole dollars' worth of quarters before spitting out those ridiculous pictures. They roomed together on the trip starting their freshman year, almost a month ago. They lay awake talking and laughed so hard their sides hurt.

It didn't seem fair. If Ashley had just kept her mouth shut, maybe things would have been different.

For a moment, Jasmín allowed herself to wonder if Ashley really told the truth.

"Not a chance," Jasmín said aloud. How else would The Moderator have known her real name?

Her phone buzzed. A waiting message.

How are you playing?

Hardball. And I'm going to win.

We'll see, Jasmín. We'll see.

Chapter 57

The Moderator sat in the driver's seat of his silver Windstar van. An evening breeze stirred the spots of light from the street lamp. On a sleepy evening in late summer, no one would think to notice another minivan parked alongside the curb. Cookie sat up in the passenger seat, her tongue lolling from the side of her mouth. The Moderator raised a pair of binoculars and studied the house across the street. Ashley was moving upstairs.

He dropped the binoculars into his lap as a car passed. He already knew her habits. He knew her family history. He knew the route her driver took to school every day. He knew the names of all her teachers. Thanks to Jasmín, he even knew which underwear she usually wore on Fridays. Kinky, but effective leverage should the need arise.

The Moderator smiled, pleased with himself.

Chapter 58

Officer Elise Trakney walked down to the passenger platform at the Florin train station and looked around. Nobody was there. She could smell the oil from the ties. The gravel of the railroad cut seemed to collect all the heat of August and throw it back at her.

Hoping for a breath of air to reach the sweat that tickled down her front, Elise shifted the ballistic vest. She stood at the platform and looked back toward the stairs. The chalk drawing of the white knight extending over the seven risers seemed to preside over the platform. Most of the outbound commuters probably missed it.

Elise studied the rail cut. Whoever drew the picture probably figured on another way out. A person going down to the station and coming back up without taking a train might arouse suspicion, but the Florin station didn't see many passengers to begin with. On the east side of the train stop, the parallel tracks ran under the Cooper Avenue overpass. Toward the west, it ran beneath South Market Street and then New Haven Street a block farther down. The houses and roads converged more densely to the east. Directly across the track, Cling Alley, a dead end, allowed residents access to the few houses that bordered the Amtrak property just above the cut. She would stop there next.

Officer Trakney walked west alongside the track. Up ahead, rail signal lights mounted on a galvanized, cantilevered pole glowed red from within their black hoods. Dirt trails ran down to the track on the west side of the South Market Bridge from the road. Above her sat the infrequently used parking area at the back of an auto shop.

She walked back toward the platform and saw a young man staring at the graffiti. Great, Elise thought, kid reporter.

"Hi, Chip. Can I help you?" Dry smile.

"Wow. That's freaky." The senior gestured toward the drawing. He was obviously excited. Elise didn't blame him. Until recently, he only wrote about food drives and funerals. The popcorn festival hosted at the local park had been the highlight of his first six months with the Gazette. This was real news. It wouldn't last. Pretty soon the county paper would get wind of it, and people would be reading about it from someone else.

"You know anything about this?" Officer Trakney asked the question.

"No. I've heard kids talking at school since my last article on the school board meeting. Most think it is just some kind of a prank."

"Most?"

"Well, there are a few hot heads dumb enough to say what they think about African-Americans, but most don't care. Besides, there aren't that many black kids in school and after a few weeks, we forget that they're black, and we're white. We're more worried about the next algebra test or the latest viral clip on You Tube." Chip raised his camera and got a vertical shot of the staircase. Then he zoomed in on the hooded eyes.

"Any ideas who would want to do this?" Officer Trakney asked.

"Nah. Most kids today have to be taught about the Ku Klux Klan. We all thought that stuff was history."

"Me, too. Come on, let's go up."

Chip led the way up the stairs.

"You know, Chip. Whoever did this probably just wanted to create a sensation." Elise looked at Chip's fluorescent green shoelaces in his canvas high tops.

"I know." He stopped at the top until she came up beside him. "Let me guess. You don't want me to print these pictures?"

"Something like that," she said.

"Ha! Sorry. This is golden." He patted his digital SLR. "Besides, I think I have the right to exercise my freedom of speech just like anyone else."

"Yep," she watched him walk away, "the freedom to be stupid."

Officer Trakney walked over to one of the township maintenance guys waiting in his air-conditioned pickup. His window slid down as she approached.

"You find anything?"

"No. Go ahead and wash it off. I'm done down there."

"Will do." He got out and pulled a power sprayer back toward him before hefting it down onto the parking lot.

"Hey, if you see any more reporters," she said, "would you hose them down, too?"

The maintenance guy gave her a thumbs-up.

Chapter 59

Chase Hikeman got in after making his circuit around town. The route usually included the local library, if it was open, and ended at the convenience store in town. He almost never saw Ashley on weekdays, and without any other friends, he needed some way to pass the time.

Chase managed to befriend several of the old folks in town and even was invited once into the Florin Historical Society to see their collection. The society purchased an older building and remodeled the top half into an apartment and converted the lower rooms into a place where they could host monthly meetings, run sessions on local history and display their collection of artifacts. Mable Ray answered all his questions.

She showed him a collection of photographs taken before the installation of the storm drains. She happened to mention the system of tunnels and rooms under the southern part of the town, and it was this that had led Chase to look for early maps.

He climbed the stairs up to his second floor apartment. It was already nine and his mother might even be home. The linoleum in the stairway was chipped badly when a couple of tenants dragged a filing cabinet up to their apartment.

He followed the scratch marks out into the hallway that ran between the street side and back side units. Here and there, he could smell cigarette smoke leaking out from underneath doors. Of course, officially, no one was allowed to smoke in the units, but it happened all the time, and so long as folks paid their rent, the landlord never came around.

Down the hall, a couple of kids on their scooters spilled out of an apartment. Their mother screamed something after them, and they split. Chase stopped in front of his own door to listen.

A light was on inside and there were voices.

Voices in the hallway were one thing. That happened all the time, especially in the winter or on rainy days when the moms couldn't kick their kids outside. But voices inside his apartment made him scared.

Chase hated to admit it. He knew why the men came over. Sometimes his mother would apologize; most often she just acted like he didn't exist when he tried to sneak in. The men with her didn't always feel the same way.

He reached for the door knob and stopped. His first thought was how quiet and clean the church sanctuary had been. Maybe he could slip inside and stay there instead.

Chase turned and walked back toward the stairs. He wished he had picked up his big flashlight from his bedroom, but he wasn't going in there. The penlight he kept with him would have to do.

White mayflies swarmed around the humming yellow light over the parking lot. Hundreds rested on the windows of cars, and Chase stopped to examine one closely. He picked it up by its upraised wings, turned it upside down to see its underbelly then put it back. The dumb creature didn't even bother to fly away.

"Not me." Chase said. "I'm not sticking around here tonight."

He jaywalked across Main Street and headed down toward the footpath along the creek. Eventually it would take him to the house at the bottom end of Barbara Street. He could hide there, easy enough.

Chapter 60

Rosalyn Faraj stood in the window, breathing in the fresh air. The overnight temperature was supposed to drop, so she opened the window and turned on the ceiling. So long as the wind wasn't blowing from a nearby chicken farm, Rosalyn liked the smell of earth and mulch and summer.

Jared had gone upstairs to bed hours ago. His actual school year would start in just a few days. Some of the boys from the team came over to visit, and Jared seemed to be settling in. She wished she could say the same for herself.

Her conversation with Pastor Blithe had confirmed her fears. The prospect that people here lived by hate surprised her. She hadn't seen it. Not like her daddy, for sure. He had told her what it had been like, growing up in a place where some of the white folks got real nasty when they put on that white hood and gown. Of course, he hadn't told her those stories until he lay in the hospital, waiting to die.

It took her daddy until then to pass those stories along. His mind failed him early on. Rosalyn and Adam traveled down to Mississippi to sit in the hospital. Then the hospice. She remembers watching him talk, his glassy eyes staring off into space like he was living again in another time. Maybe he was. Sometimes he started trembling and sweat streamed down the sides of his face. Rosalyn didn't want to hear the stories, but she couldn't leave him alone in that place, not with him reliving all the horror. Other times her daddy would cry out for his own mama.

Even though Rosalyn had never lived the horror her daddy faced in a racist South, somehow she inherited his fear.

She'd been called names before, but her mama would always remind her. "Never give back what you get, or you're no better than they are." Once she told her mother she didn't want to be better, she wanted to get even. Funny how you end up repeating what your mama says, she thought. Just yesterday she gave Jared the same advice. He just wrinkled up his face and asked, "What are you talking about mama? How am I supposed to play football like that?" Everything was about football with that boy.

Rosalyn sighed.

She climbed into the empty bed and pulled up the sheet. If Adam wasn't around, she didn't sleep well at all. Not that she told him. Adam had enough on his plate with his job. He didn't seem to think there was anything to worry about.

She kicked off the sheet again and waited for the fan breeze to cool her skin through her silk pajamas. Adam was working late tonight. A couple of nights a week he took the car to the county's main train station because the late night trains didn't make a stop in Florin. The squared green numbers on the digital clock blinked over to 11. Unconsciously, she listened for his car to pull in the drive way, but he wouldn't be there for another half hour, at least. Outside there was the faint stirring sound of a breeze, and Rosalyn looked for the sheers to start moving in the window.

Instead, she heard a voice calling to her. It sounded like it came from someone on the sidewalk. "Blackie."

Rosalyn grabbed the sheet and pulled it up.

"Blackie." The voice moved closer, creeping around the side of the house, hiding among the white pine trees that screened the side of their property. Her hand slid across the bed for the phone.

The demonic sound floated in through her window, alternately louder and softer. It sounded forced or strained or other-worldly. She couldn't tell.

The phone slipped out of her hand and fell to the carpeted floor. Without breathing, she inched to the edge of the bed, feeling around the floor until she touched the hard corner. Clammy fingers clung to the phone.

She slipped out of the bed, crawled away from the window and out into the hall. Pulling the phone close to her chest, she dialed 911.

"911 operator. Do you need ambulance, fire, or police?"

"Police." Rosalyn Faraj whispered into the phone.

"What is your location?"

"I'm on West Oak Alley. Near the park. Number 122."

"Are you in danger?"

"Yes. I think so." In her mind she could hear her daddy crying out for his mama. She choked back the panic. "I think so. There's someone outside my house."

Chapter 61

The emergency operator relayed the call to Officer Ken Dixon, who punched the lights and pulled a U-turn to head back toward town. He could feel a rush of adrenaline hit his system. Stay alert. Keep your eyes open. Get the bad guy. He radioed back to the station and requested back up. With any luck they would arrive at the same time.

"This is Officer Dixon. I'm going in dark and quiet."

"The caller is reporting a voice outside her window. First floor. East side."

Dixon stopped the cruiser on the far side of Memorial Park and hit the ground at a run. He cut through the park, using the trees as much as possible to screen himself from view. He saw Officer Trakney roll in farther down Oak Alley. Headlights off. She signaled to him with one blink of her flashlight. They converged on house number 122. No cars were parked directly out front. A silver minivan sat on the opposite side of the street facing them. No active players.

Elise motioned that she was going to take the side nearest her. He undid the snap and pulled his revolver. Pushing his back against the garage door, he eased himself around. Shadowy pine trees extended in a line away from the road between the house and the one next to it. Too dark. Dixon turned on his flashlight and flushed boughs of the trees with white light. Nothing. He hurried now, searching the shadows, walking the perimeter of the house.

Then he heard a voice near his shoulder. "Blackie"

He spun around to find no one behind him. Something gleamed black in the glow of his light. He moved in and shone his light directly on an object resting on the window sill.

Officer Trakney approached. "What did you find?"

"A recorder." Dixon nodded toward the house, and Elise holstered her weapon and went to ring the front door bell. She radioed dispatch to issue the all-clear. The emergency operator would relay the message to Mrs. Faraj inside the house.

Dixon pulled a pen from his pocket and poked the off button before following Elise toward the front door.

Elise knocked lightly on the door. The porch light blinked on and the door opened a crack.

"Mrs. Faraj? Everything is clear."

Rosalyn Faraj pulled back the door and stared out at the two officers. She wore a white terry cloth robe and was obviously shaken.

"Did you find him?" she asked.

"It was a recording. Someone placed a microcassette recorder on your window sill."

"Excuse me?"

"No one is out here, ma'am. It was only a recording. Do you mind if we come in?"

"Of course." Rosalyn let the way into the kitchen and offered them the bar stools at the kitchen counter. The officers declined the seats.

"Are you alone here, Mrs. Faraj?" Elise asked.

"No. My son, Jared is asleep upstairs."

"How old is he?"

"Seventeen."

"Do you know of anyone who would want to play a prank on you or your son?"

"A prank? That's what you call this?" Mrs. Faraj bristled. "And if they burn a cross in my grass tomorrow, do you want me to call that a prank as well?"

They heard the garage door open. "That's my husband. He's just getting back from work."

"Where does he work?" Elise Trakney took down a few notes.

"He works at Temple University."

"Doing?"

"Adam is a teaching doctor."

Dr. Faraj stepped into the laundry room from the garage and stopped cold when he saw the police.

"Is everything okay?" he asked. "Where's Jared?"

"He's upstairs in bed. Sleeping I hope," said Mrs. Faraj. "I called the police."

"Officer Trakney." Elise stepped forward to shake his hand. "This is Officer Dixon."

"We responded to an emergency call from this address, but we believe everything is clear," Officer Dixon said.

"What happened?"

"A recording device was placed outside your window with a racial slur on some kind of looping message." Dixon looked over at Mrs. Faraj. "There's no need to feel embarrassed. You were right to call it in."

"Dr. Faraj, do you know of anyone who might be trying to intimidate you or your family?"

Dr. Faraj put his keys on the counter and went over to his wife. "No. We've only just moved to the area. I commute into Philadelphia for work."

"Do you leave from the Florin station?" Elise Trakney thumbed back through her notes to see who called in the graffiti.

"I do. And yes, I saw the drawing." He looked as his wife. "I didn't want to tell you about it. Didn't want you to be afraid."

"And do you believe the threat was directed toward you?" Trakney asked.

"What threat? What are you talking about?" Rosalyn looked hard at her husband.

"There was a drawing of a Ku Klux Klan member at the train stop with the words 'leave before you get hurt' written above it." Dr. Faraj pulled on his tie and undid the top button.

"You didn't want me to be afraid?" Her voice rose, incredulous, but she hushed herself. "What about our son?"

"Ma'am," Officer Trakney interrupted. "We have no reason to believe these threats are anything more than a couple of prejudiced kids."

"Prejudiced kids kill black boys, Officer. Don't you dare make an assumption at the expense of my family."

"I appreciate your concern, Mrs. Faraj," Dixon intervened. "We are looking closely at this situation and have already consulted with our chief in light of the rumors around about a hate group forming at the local high school. It is out of character for this area, but we're taking it seriously anyway. That said, we are also careful not to give unnecessary publicity to someone who just wants to make inflammatory statements."

"Do you know of any reason why someone would want to threaten you or your family, Dr. Faraj?" Officer Trakney asked again.

Mrs. Faraj crossed her arms. "You mean *apart* from the fact that we're Muslim, black and well-off?"

"I'm sorry, I'm not trying to ignore the racial nature of the threats; I'm merely trying to isolate a possible suspect."

"We're aware of how this must make you feel," Dixon said. "We are disappointed that this has happened. You can rest assured that we intend to find out who is doing this and take every legal action against them."

"Thank you, officers. We appreciate your time." The doctor leaned heavily on the counter.

"I'll take another look around outside to see if there is anything we missed." Dixon said. "We'll take the device down to the station and see if we can get anything helpful from it."

Mrs. Faraj began to calm down. "Any chance you'll get prints off it?"

"There's a chance. If there are prints, it is unlikely we'll find a match in our system." Trakney pulled a card from her pocket and placed it next to the doctor's keys. "We'll keep an eye on your place. Please call us if you need anything or have any more information for us."

Dixon followed her out the door and pulled an evidence bag from one of his pockets. "I'll make another round before I leave." She nodded and walked back to her car.

Dixon's light probed the mulch near the window. Kids these days were smart enough to wipe off their fingerprints or use gloves, and they were smart enough not to leave footprints in the mulch. Touching only a corner, he slid the recorder into the bag and gave it a sniff before he closed the top.

Chapter 62

"Were you in the catacombs?" Chase found Ashley on her way out of services. He looked awkward standing there waiting for her in his everyday clothes. People looked at him with something like pity. Probably because he didn't believe in God. Chase gave his glasses a bump back into place and walked up to her.

"What are you talking about?" Ashley stepped out of the flow of people leaving the building.

"You know, the cave. Have you been back there?" Chase looked her right in the eyes.

Ashley glanced away. "Of course not. I thought we agreed not to go back in there. You know, how it would ruin 'historic artifacts' and all that."

"You sure?" Chase asked again.

Ashley felt her face get hot with the lies. "I'm sure." She managed to look him in the face again, but felt her heart throbbing in her head. It was perfect. She had known he wouldn't be able to stay out of there. "Why?" she asked. Even to her, the casual question felt forced.

Chase looked off down the street. "Because I found something. I have to go to the police."

"What?" The pounding grew louder inside her head.

"There's something there they'll need to see."

"You can't do that. We weren't supposed to be in there in the first place."

"I know."

"If you go to the police, we'll probably get arrested for trespassing or something."

"People don't get arrested for trespassing."

Ashley swore. "If my dad finds out I've been in there with you, he'll kill me."

"You just swore," Chase said.

"So?"

"It's a Sunday. You swore on a Sunday. Doesn't that tick God off?"

"Chase!" Ashley almost shouted. "You're missing the point. You can't go to the police. I mean it."

"I have to. I think they'll be lenient with me because I'm going to them."

"What makes you think they'll go easy on you?" Ashley asked.

"Because I'm interested in preserving historic artifacts."

"Well. They may go easy with you, but my dad will kill me."

"He won't really kill you." Chase didn't have much space for drama.

"Chase, you can't." She reached out and put a hand on his chest. She had never touched him quite like that before.

He was adamant. "Look. You can come with me, or you can stay home. It doesn't really matter."

Chase turned and walked away.

With any luck, she thought, he won't mention that she went along. Either way, it was all working out much better than she expected.

Chapter 63

Mable Ray lived on the far side of town in a tiny house built in the early 1950's. The house was young for the town, but it faded quickly, and peeling red paint made the asbestos siding look furry. Chase noticed, but then he noticed almost everything. It didn't hurt that he liked architecture. Architecture was a way of seeing how other people lived. He noticed the rhododendron bushes reaching across the front step. It didn't look like the woman saw much company.

Chase had never visited her before. He only knew where she lived because he saw her address on an envelope she used as a bookmark the day he visited the Florin Historical Society. Visitors didn't frequent the place, so he figured she got a lot of reading done.

He paced back and forth out front. He didn't know if she was married. Generally, Chase preferred women. Men scared him. A couple of cars went past, but Chase couldn't make himself knock on the door.

Chase saw a watery copy of the neighborhood gazette and picked it up. A few pincher bugs crawled out, and he rattled them off. Holding it by the corner Chase carried it up the walk with some vague idea about asking if she dropped it, how he could probably dry it out for her if she needed it, how he spilled juice on a book once and managed to get it dry—

"Chase Hikeman. What are you doing with that piece of trash?" Mable Ray stood on the driveway beside the house wiping her hands on the belly of her apron.

He dropped it. "I was just walking past your place and saw it laying there in the grass and—"

"Nonsense. You've been pacing back and forth out here for 15 minutes. No one ever uses that door. Come around to the back here."

Chase obeyed and cut across the grass. "I'm sorry to disturb you at home."

"Speaking of which, how did you know where I live?" Mable Ray put her hands on her hips.

She was always like this. Short. Direct. Pointed. The perfect retired librarian.

"I saw it on an envelope you used as a bookmark."

"Well then, I guess you'll just have to come in and join me for lunch. Tuna melts." She turned and led him into the house through the side door. "When it comes to tuna and cheese, I'm a master chef."

Chase stopped just outside the door.

"What's the matter? You afraid I'm going to bite you or something?"

"No. It's just I've never been invited into someone else's house before." Even Ashley only met him at his place or the park.

Mable Ray studied him for a minute, then said, "Well, you'll just have to get used it now, won't you."

"Yes, ma'am." Chase followed her into the house.

A stove crowded between yellow metal cabinets. Mable Ray dropped another piece of bread into a stainless steel toaster and pushed down the button. "You came just in time. I was about to eat without you."

Chase nodded dumbly but couldn't find anything to say. Mable Ray smelled like her house, or her house smelled like her. He wasn't sure how it worked. His own home just smelled like cigarette smoke. A sunflower dishtowel hung in front of the oven. Mable Ray looked him over again and nodded as if answering her own question.

"I was also thinking I need to mix up a batch of brownies this afternoon. Wash your hands over there and get down a mixing bowl for me."

Suddenly Chase found himself pouring and mixing and cracking eggs and fishing out broken bits of eggshell.

"Not with your fingers. You'll never get it with your fingers." Mable Ray peered down at the shard of eggshell he'd managed to drop. "Well now, we have two options. We can leave it in there and hope the other person gets it, or we can fish it out."

Chase gave her a worried look. "Let's fish it out."

"I agree. Grab one half of the shell and use it to fish out the pieces."

"Why not a spoon?"

"Go ahead and try it."

Chase tried, but the piece kept running away from the spoon. Then he picked up the empty egg shell and the broken bit came right out with it. Chase stared at the edge of the egg shell for a while, trying to determine what had made the difference. He decided he would need to slip an eggshell into the science lab and take a look at it under the dissection scope.

Mable Ray turned on the oven and poured them both a cup of coffee. "Milk and sugar?"

"Sure." Chase tried to sound like coffee was a normal part of his life.

She handed him a cup. "Now sit down over here and tell me what I can do for you."

Chase deliberated, studying his coffee. "Ms. Ray, I need to go to the police."

Mable Ray's mug stopped at her lips.

His eyes blinked at her from behind the lenses. "Will you go with me?"

Chapter 64

Ashley peered out across the grassy lawn from her bedroom window. Mrs. Hansel had just arrived back from lunch and walked up the path toward the church. As usual, Renee Hansel was beautiful. Even Ashley noticed. The woman smiled at someone in the church doorway whom Ashley couldn't see, but she knew to be her father.

"Gotcha." Ashley extended the remote toward the window and pushed the button, switching the camera to standby. It would start recording the moment it detected movement.

She hadn't thought it would work from this far away, but she'd tested it beforehand.

Ashley dropped the remote into her desk drawer and paced around the room, trying to find something to do to keep her mind off what was happening over at the church. She felt cagey. Wanted to move. Didn't want to think. The computer blinked on when she touched the mouse. Ashley's fingers hovered over the keys. Instead, she grabbed her phone, left the house through the back door and started walking. She wanted to brag. She punched in a phone number The Moderator had given her and sent a message.

I'm close. I'm going to win that F'N pot of gold.

Then she waited. Two minutes.

We'll see, PK. We'll see.

Chapter 65

Ken Dixon parked the police cruiser alongside the road under a linden tree. Officer Trakney had actually been en route to follow up on the call but was diverted to deal with a traffic incident. Trakney radioed Dixon to give him the address. He picked up his notepad and glanced at the number on the mailbox.

He walked up the front walk and knocked at the door. A woman with a pinched face and a grey head appeared on the drive beside the house.

"Are you Officer Dixon?"

"Yes, I am. Are you Mrs. Hikeman?"

"No. I'm Mable Ray. I'm Chase's—I'm just a friend of his. Come in over here." She stopped him before they went inside. "Thanks for making a house call. Chase will be much more comfortable talking with you here, I'm sure."

Dixon followed Mable Ray into the kitchen. "It smells good in here."

"Those are brownies, and this is Chase Hikeman." She pointed to a young teenager with ratty brown hair and coke-bottle glasses. The temple tips on the boy's glasses wrapped around the back of his ears, making them stick out.

"Hi, Chase. I'm officer Dixon." He reached out to shake the boy's hand. It was cold.

Officer Dixon settled himself at the kitchen table across from them. A legal pad rested in front. "So, Mr. Hikeman, have we met before?"

"No, sir." Chase gave his glasses a bump.

"How old are you?"

"I'm almost fifteen. Ninth grade this year."

"You go to Florin High?"

"Yes, sir."

"Where do you live?" Dixon asked.

Chase Hikeman squirmed in his seat and looked over at Mable Ray. "Across town."

"It would really help me if I could put an address down," Dixon said.

"I live in the Terraces." He sighed and ran his fingers along the edge of the table, trying to hide his embarrassment.

"So what can I do for you, Mr. Hikeman."

"I want to report a crime. Two, actually. Trespassing. That's the first one. I did that one." Chase looked down at his fingernails.

Dixon glanced at Mable Ray. She was staring at Chase.

"The second one is defacing a historic monument." The boy looked up at him through his glasses and added, "But I didn't do that one."

"Okay. I'm glad you came to see me." Officer Dixon wanted to put the boy at ease. He was obviously scared.

"Can you tell me where these crimes took place?"

"Yes, sir. Down at the bottom end of Barbara Street. I don't know the house number."

"Can you describe the house?"

"It's a stone building that's been divided up into a bunch of different apartments. I think it was built in the early 1800's. Ms. Mable has some maps from 1830 and it was already there then."

"I'm the curator of the local historical society," Mable added by way of clarification.

"I'm familiar with the house." Dixon made another note on his pad.

"Is this house where the historic monument is located?"

"Actually, the house is the historic monument, sort of," Chase said.

"Why don't you tell me about it?"

Dixon took notes while the boy talked. Occasionally Dixon asked a question, but Chase's eye for detail was quite remarkable.

When he finished, Dixon glanced through his notes and asked, "So, who went in there with you?"

"No one." Chase replied. "I went by myself."

"Funny thing," Dixon tapped at his paper. "You said you noticed 'our' footprints had been erased by the water dripping in from the recent rains." He looked up at the boy. "Did you take someone in there with you?"

Chase looked across at Mable Ray. She said nothing but shifted her head to the side and stared back at the boy.

"Well. Okay. I took a girl in there."

Ken Dixon's eyebrows went up.

"It wasn't like that. She's not my girlfriend or anything, though I wouldn't mind if she was." Chase allowed a sheepish smile.

"What's her name?"

"Ashley Blithe." He spoke the name softly.

"Why didn't you tell me about her before?" Officer Dixon jotted the name on his paper.

Chase furrowed his brow and looked at the officer. "She's really afraid of her dad finding out about this. He's a pastor, and I guess he takes a pretty dim view of sin and stuff like that."

Officer Dixon stifled a chuckle with a cough.

"Do you think she has anything do with what you found in this underground room?" Dixon tried to pass the question off casually.

"No way! I've never heard her say anything bad about black people." Chase pushed his glasses up hard against his face and squinted through them at the officer.

"Well, like you said, two crimes were committed here. If you had nothing to do with the vandalism, the property owners may not press charges."

"It was really my idea to go in there in the first place. She's cool like that; she likes exploring and learning stuff. Not like most girls. Is she going to get into trouble?" The boy's voice pleaded.

"I'm not sure if she'll get in trouble or not. We're going to need to talk to her."

"If she goes to the station to talk to you, would her father have to find out?" Chase asked.

"Again, that depends, but if she came to us, that would be a step in the right direction."

Chase's shoulders sagged. "She's going to be pissed."

Chapter 66

"You're an ass, Chase." Ashley said. "I knew you wouldn't be able to keep me out of this."

"It is a historic artifact. Besides, do you want to live in a town where the Ku Klux Klan is sneaking around ruining all the best hiding places?"

She looked at him crossly. "So what do I have to do?"

"The police officer said he'd need to talk to you."

"You're kidding."

"Not kidding. If you head down to the station tomorrow after school, he won't have to come to your home to interview you," Chase said.

Ashley put her hands on her hips and leaned over so her face was close to his, "You owe me."

Chapter 67

Officer Dixon met Chip Perry at the Barbara Street property Sunday afternoon after contacting the landlord.

"I still can't believe you called me," he said. The lanky youth yanked his hat down over curls that threatened to escape. The kid probably didn't sit still in class, but he was an excellent photographer and a tolerable writer.

The police needed someone who could drive a camera. Besides, Officer Dixon liked to give the local seniors a taste of real life. Actually, Chip's writing tended to be factual to the point of dry. Perfect for this situation. The officers argued briefly about the merit of going public, but Chief Gregson wanted to increase public vigilance.

"We're hoping you can get some decent pictures in there. It doesn't get much darker than that."

"No problem. I brought an auxiliary flash and a battery-powered flood to give us some light. It should be plenty based on the room dimensions you gave me."

"Can I help you carry some of that?"

"Sure thing." Chip handed the officer a tripod and a canvas bag with the flash.

"Remember, we can't touch anything when we're inside."

With the help of Dixon's mag light, they manhandled the equipment through the opening to the secret chamber. Once they entered the main room, Chip set up his flood and switched it on. The entire chamber popped with light.

The walls were covered with racial threats painted in blaze yellow. The pictures hanging in plastic protectors showed victims of heinous crimes. Violent, bloody and cruel.

Chip stood staring at the gallery of hatred. "This is freaky." A white sheet with eye holes cut in it hung from an old iron hook in the wall.

Once Chip set to work on getting his pictures, he was all business. He situated the tripod where he could get a wide angle shot of the room. Officer Dixon held the auxiliary flash connected to Chip's camera by a long wire that looked like the curled cord on a tethered phone.

"Hold that higher and point it toward the back corner. Good, right there." Light exploded, leaving floating spots of flash in their eyes.

"Good. Let's do that again. Angle it toward the ceiling."

Dixon adjusted the flash. "Here?" Dixon shielded his eyes.

"Yes." The flash erupted again.

After 15 minutes Chip Perry had photographed everything.

"Do you know who did this?" Chip asked as he packed his camera back into its case.

"Not yet. Have you heard anything more over at the school?" Dixon retracted the telescoping legs on the tripod and flicked off some mud sticking to it.

"There are some kids talking about who they think is in on it. It is kind of a sensation right now. Everyone has an opinion. Everyone thinks they're right." Chip stood up from his bag and looked at Dixon. "No one really knows anything. Kids talk when they don't know something. When they really do know something, they whisper."

Dixon smiled. "Sounds like we can make a detective out of you yet."

"You're sure I'm allowed to publish these pictures?"

"Sure thing. I've already contacted the county paper to let them know we'll be sending them the story. They wanted to send a reporter over, but I told them you would cover it. You'll have to get it in before 10 p.m. to make the deadline."

Chip Perry's smile stretched across his thin face. "Officer Dixon, you are a cool dude."

"Yes, I am. Now get to work."

Chapter 68

Ashley's mom managed to boil up perogies with some spaghetti sauce. Lisa had probably helped her, but at least for a while, it felt like a normal night. Then her dad left for a board meeting and her mom returned to her room. Ashley slipped into the church.

The wooden door went shut with a definitive clunk that startled her. The thick stone walls seemed to close out the rest of the world, as if the space inside the building somehow belonged to another time and place. She walked between the pews down the center aisle. She used to play wedding in here while her dad worked. He didn't mind so long as she didn't touch the organ. Their church was one of the few that boasted its own pipe organ. The pipes rose like thin brass smoke stacks with funny lids. She didn't know how much it cost, but her father suggested it would be a bad idea to touch it, and as long as he let her play wedding, the old organ didn't hold much appeal.

Some Sundays a visiting music student from the local state college would play a few pieces. Ashley wasn't a fan of organ music, per se, but the sound seemed to rise out of that other world, and it touched something in her.

Ashley stopped at the rectory door and checked behind her. No one was there. She was just nervous. The thought of being caught and the thought of what she might find on the surveillance video made her jumpy. Just get in there, get the disk and get out, she told herself.

Jasmín had agreed to preview it. She would give it to her at school the next morning. Ashley didn't want to watch it herself. She didn't want to see her dad with another woman.

Chapter 69

Chip Perry did it up right. If Chief Gregson wanted people to be aware of the situation, that's exactly what he would get. After writing up a pithy cover story on the re-emergence of a white supremacist group in sleepy Florin, he emailed a copy to the local television news station and attached the best of his pictures. Chip sent another copy to the county paper along with a couple of other photos.

The entire county woke up to a blurb on the front page of the morning papers. The story made the 6 a.m. newscast and the phone at the Florin police department started ringing before the shift change. The story swept up a dust storm of outrage. The fact that the story seemed to highlight Florin High School as the epicenter of the hate group didn't do much to endear Chip Perry to the building principal, but Chip weathered the storm with a calm resolve. After all, this was the pinnacle of high school journalism. A group of disenfranchised youth joined around him, shielding him from institutional persecution, finding a sudden heady power in the constitutional right to free speech.

Chapter 70

Adam Faraj saw the story on the morning news long before Rosalyn got up. He knew he wouldn't be able to hide it from her. She had been on edge ever since she heard about all this. At first he tried to downplay it. But she wasn't sleeping and her fear began to spill over into her dreams. He told her they would leave if things got worse. Before someone got hurt. This was the last straw. As soon as she heard the news, she would call the real estate agent.

Adam spread out his prayer mat. He pulled his tagiyah down over his hair. The prayer cap had been purchased by a friend of his who visited Morocco recently on vacation. Not many of Adam's friends would have been as considerate. The gold embroidery thread blended nicely with the gray. He knelt toward the East and began his first rak'a, but he couldn't concentrate. Instead, his mouth fell silent, and Adam just knelt there trying to make sense out of everything.

The move here had seemed right. They easily found a buyer for their house in Philadelphia. Rosalyn talked up the benefits of moving to the country. How Jared would have more opportunities in schools, how they wouldn't have to worry so much about the constant pressure facing black kids in the city.

Adam agreed to move to the country after a trauma case involving a 13 year-old with a gunshot wound. The bullet scrambled the boy's insides. Adam and his student doctor labored hours in surgery trying to figure out what piece belonged where. Medicine was supposed to be scientific, but he felt like he was putting a puzzle together without defined edges. Every piece had to be tried some place until it look like a reasonable match.

After seven hours in surgery, the boy died. No one expected it. He just died. Right there on the table. It was as if the violence, the drugs, the anger of the city just sucked the life out of him.

He remembered the nurses removing his surgical gown. He dropped his glove into the red, bio hazard bag and washed under steaming water. Thick soapy lather. He walked out of the surgery to find the boy's mother and sister alone in a corner of the waiting room.

Adam rubbed his face with his hands, trying to clear away the memory of the woman's grief. He restarted his prayer again, forcing himself to concentrate on the words.

The thought of leaving Rosalyn for the day made him tense. He got up, rolled up the rug, and took off his prayer cap. Time to go to work. It promised to be another late night.

Chapter 71

Officers Dixon and Trakney sat in the conference room reviewing their notes and photographs. Preston Farwick sat at his work station nearby. The two officers found no substantive leads on the graffiti at the train station. The drawing was crude mostly because it was divided up to fit across the backs of several stairs.

"Have you spoken with this girl yet—what's her name again?"

"Ashley. No, not yet. Chase Hikeman suggested she might pay us a visit this afternoon."

"What do you think?"

"I think she's an unlikely suspect. According to Hikeman, Ashley doesn't exactly fit the profile for hate crimes."

"So what's the motive?"

"None, that I can think of."

"Aside from rumors circulating of a resurgence of the Klan, we have three separate incidents and nothing to link any of them together beyond relative location."

Ken Dixon picked up his coffee and held it under his nose while he thought. Suddenly he set it down and snapped his fingers. "It was a girl."

"Who?"

"Whoever put the recording at the Faraj residence."

"How do you know?" Trakney asked.

"I almost forgot. I gave the recorder a sniff before I put it in the bag. It had definitely been handled by a girl."

"No kidding," Trakney said. "You're really sniffing evidence?"

"Hey, whatever works."

"Just make sure you don't sniff all the evidence we collect."

They laughed.

"Seriously, though. We have a girl at the scene of the Faraj residence, and one in the cave."

"Do you think she is working alone?"

"Hard to know; she'll never tell us."

Preston Farwick leaned back in his chair. A pencil wedged behind his ear. His fingers absently teased his hair into untidy bunches while he concentrated. "You could search her cell phone. You know, pull phone log, text messages, browsing history."

"We'd have to get a search warrant for that, I think." Dixon looked at Trakney. "You think the judge would go for that?"

Trakney shrugged. "He likes me. I'll ask him. I don't know if he'll go for the 'smell' connection."

"Worth a try. Farwick, how long would it take you to get that information off her phone?"

Preston stared at the ceiling and scratched his head. "Depends on the phone. I can probably have it done in about 15 minutes or less."

Elise Trakney glanced at her watch. "If I hustle over, we might be able to get the judge to write us a warrant before she comes today. If she has her phone with her, Preston can 'borrow' it for a while and then send it home."

"Go for it," Dixon replied. "Preston, you going to be around this afternoon to do that?"

"I can be. Not like I've got much else to do."

"Since you're clearances have come in, you're even officially legal." Ken Dixon smiled. "You make good on this, and you just might get a real job yet."

Preston Farwick grinned. "Now *that* is a happy thought."

Chapter 72

The real estate agent pulled the house details from the previous listing agent. It made her job easier. She didn't have to bother getting all the room dimensions and tax specs on the property.

"I'm sorry to hear things haven't worked out here for you." She pulled a thick disclosure statement from a blue folder and set it down on the kitchen counter. "This is hard for all of us."

Rosalyn didn't care about the paperwork. She wanted her family safe. They located several properties in central Jersey within a reasonable commute to the university hospital. She wanted out.

"You'll both have to sign the papers, but I'll go ahead and put the sign out while I'm here. I can even get an MLS number assigned to the property. Just have your husband fax over the paperwork tonight. I'll be in the office late anyway."

"Thank you." Rosalyn picked up the pen and signed the paper.

"How long do you think it will take to sell the property?" Rosalyn asked.

"It's hard to say. The market has been all over the place lately. As soon as we get the signatures from your husband, we can run the listing online. Most local papers close their weekend advertising on Thursday, so assuming I get your disclosure statements before I leave the office tonight, I'll make sure our secretary sends the ads out first thing tomorrow morning." She gathered up the rest of her papers and slid them into her attaché case.

Chapter 73

Their van driver dropped them at the corner. The sisters shouldered their bags and headed home.

"What are you doing tonight?" Ashley asked.

"I'm going over to Darren's."

"I thought he had swim practice."

"He does, but he'll be home after supper."

Ashley stopped on the curb at the corner and waited for Lisa to catch up. She looked across the street at the rectory and the church. "You ever get tired of living in a church?"

"Yes. Except we don't live *in* a church."

"Feels like it." Ashley looked up the street and saw the new blue and white realtor sign in the strip of grass between the sidewalk and street in front of Dr. Faraj's house. Her eyes got wide, and she bit her tongue to keep in the excitement. Lisa went on ahead, so Ashley pulled out her phone and dawdled on the sidewalk long enough to send a text to The Moderator's phone. This would make her Level 4.

The house is up for sale!

She wondered where The Moderator lived. The zip code was unfamiliar. Must be some other state. Ashley made a mental note to look it up later and slipped the phone into the pocket of her kilt. Why did the guy give her a phone number if he wanted the game to be so hush-hush? The phone vibrated against her leg. She pulled it out.

"Yes!" Ashley jumped off the sidewalk squarely into a rain puddle at the side of the road. "Yes, yes, yes!" She stomped around in it, splashing water on her shoes waving her phone triumphantly in the air. Ashley smiled and looked at the reply again.

Way to go PK. You win the POG.

Chapter 74

The Florin police station sat across from another church along Main Street. The brick building looked remarkable only in its complete lack of style. Square. Red brick. No nonsense with a couple of police cars parked out front along the curb. Ashley felt nervous. She'd never been in a police station before, but she could pull it off.

After all, she was a master of disguise. Even Chase had no idea what she was up to. This should be easy, she thought. I'm just afraid of my dad. I'm sorry I went exploring without asking for permission. I'll do anything to make it right if you'll just not tell my dad. It was a story she could sell.

She noticed a cream doorbell in the wall. It looked like a fish-eye with a cataract, she thought. "Pisces," she whispered aloud. Fish. The bell sounded like a buzzer at a swim meet, only not as loud. That makes you feel welcome, she thought.

Another buzzer sounded, and a voice from a speaker somewhere told her to come in. Ashley stood in an entry way between two doors. Thick glass separated her from the woman behind the desk. A single round communication hole with a metal vent made Ashley feel like she was in jail. Or buying tickets at the theater.

"Hi. I'm Ashley Blithe. I need to talk to Mr. Dixon."

The woman tapped something into her keyboard. "Do you have an appointment with Officer Dixon?"

"No. Well, kinda. I think a friend told him I would be stopping by."

"You will have to leave your cell phone at the desk."

This was a surprise. She slipped it from her pocket. The woman behind the glass pointed down, and Ashley noticed an opening below the glass she hadn't seen before.

"Silence it first, please."

Ashley touched the screen and turned off the sound, then slipped it under the glass to the woman. The secretary slid the phone into a brown envelope.

"'Ey' or 'ee' to spell your name?"

"'Ey.'" Ashley watched the woman write her name with a permanent marker on the envelope and then mark down the date and time like she was collecting evidence. The thought made her uncomfortable. She was the good guy, Ashley reminded herself. She was here to volunteer information. Police people love that.

She smiled at the woman.

"You can go through now. Turn to your right and have a seat in the waiting room. Officer Dixon will come to get you when he's ready."

The air conditioning was certainly working. Her legs immediately felt cold all the way up. She hadn't bothered to change out of her uniform. Ashley wanted the police to see that she had come over as soon as she could. She gritted her teeth as she sat down on the cold plastic cushion and tucked her fingers under her bare legs. A couple of DARE posters decorated the waiting room alongside profiles of the FBI's most wanted. Ashley studied them. Some were wanted for murder; some were child molesters on the run. Yuk.

"You know any of those people?" A police officer stood in the doorway, his hair cropped so short it stood up all over.

Ashley wrinkled her nose. "Not my type."

He chuckled. "I'm Officer Dixon. Chase said you'd be stopping by."

"I'm Ashley Blithe." She immediately felt foolish. "I guess you knew that already."

"Yes, I do. Nervous?"

"No." Ashley made a face. "Maybe a little."

"Come on, let's go back to my office. It's freezing out here."

Chapter 75

Preston Farwick slipped Ashley's cell phone from the envelope and set it on his desk. He took a deep breath and went to work. First he turned on his computer and downloaded mIQ from the Web. While it was installing, Farwick saved all Ashley's SMS messages to her SIM card.

Farwick dug in his bag until he found the right adaptor to link her phone with the USB port on his laptop. Then he went online to mIQ's website, logged in and synced her phone with his laptop. Farwick copied every email address, text, and photo on the girl's phone.

Back in his cubicle, Farwick installed the driver for the office printer. He navigated through the mIQ website where the phone data was saved and pulled up all her text messages from the last two weeks. He selected these as a group and sent them to the office printer.

The printer hummed and spit paper into the tray.

Less than 10 minutes after he started, Preston Farwick slipped the pink phone back into the envelope and returned it to the secretary with a wink. "Mission accomplished."

Chapter 76

"Am I going to get in trouble for going in there?" Ashley asked.

"That depends if the homeowners press charges. At this point, if you confess to being in there, they're going to think you are the people who made a mess of things." Officer Dixon watched her casually.

"Is it really bad?" Ashley asked.

"I'm afraid it is. I was in there this morning with the photographer."

"A photographer?" Ashley had already seen the write-up in the morning paper at the school library. It was perfect. She couldn't have asked for better.

"We have to document everything we find. Evidence, you know."

"Right." Ashley chewed absently on her cheek. She looked him in the eyes. "I can't believe people would do that kind of thing."

Chapter 77

"My parents are home." Darren met Lisa at the door.

Lisa nodded. She rarely saw them, and it was better that way. Loud outbursts interspersed with cold silence invaded the usual yawning quiet of the place when they were around.

They left the house and walked hand in hand to the cul-de-sac where the development ended and cornfields began. A mass of red-winged black birds swarmed past overhead as the two moved onto a mowed lane dividing two fields. The path turned, following a swale and eventually all but the roofs of the houses disappeared behind towering tasseled corn stalks.

Lisa reached out and put her hand low on Darren's back. He stopped and turned to her.

She bit her bottom lip gently. "We're alone now." It was a suggestion.

Darren looked away.

"Are you afraid or something? No one ever comes out here." Lisa undid the lower buttons on her shirt showing the gleam of jewelry in her navel. Darren was shy about affection, and she liked that about him.

He leaned in to kiss her but stopped and turned away.

"What's the matter?"

Darren made a fist to keep his fingers still.

"Don't you want to kiss me?"

Something was wrong. Lisa pulled back.

"No." Darren said finally. The single word deflated him.

"What are you saying?"

"It's not you. I just don't find you attractive."

Lisa felt the rush of humiliation. Shame.

"Is there someone else?" Lisa didn't want to know.

A dry wind pushed its way among the stalks making hushing noises.

Darren cried.

Lisa had never seen him cry. His tears touched her. She wanted to hold him, comfort him—rock him even.

"It's not like that," Darren said. He could hardly speak. He pressed his fists into his eyes then stood up straight. Resolved.

"I'm gay."

Lisa's legs felt wobbly. She should say something. Nothing came. Only visceral self-hatred.

Lisa turned then and ran. Grass tore at her ankles as she fled.

Chapter 78

"Find anything interesting?" Officer Dixon leaned against the partition wall of Preston Farwick's temporary desk. Farwick had returned to the office late to keep working.

"I think so." He was highlighting time signatures on the transcripts of Ashley Blithe's more interesting text conversations. "It's him again."

"Who?" Dixon asked.

"The two-minute man." Farwick handed the papers to Dixon for review.

"You think this is the same guy?"

Farwick seemed agitated at the question. "What is the likelihood of the exact same time signature as the other kids?"

Dixon glanced over the paper without responding. He looked at the phone number. "I don't recognize this zip code. Is it the same number those three other kids were calling?"

"No. This is a Wisconsin zip; I looked it up. There are any number of places online you can get a fake phone number so your own is hidden. Chances are this guy is too smart not to know that. I'm guessing he made initial contact with these kids online and then gave them different numbers."

"So much for getting a reverse phone book and calling someone over there to pick him up."

"Not likely."

"What do you make of this text?" Dixon put the papers down in front of Farwick. *"Way to go PK. You win the POG. "* Dixon read the line.

"Looks like she's been playing some kind of online game."

Dixon reviewed the lines before it. "What does that have to do with a house up for sale?" Dixon asked.

"It's probably part of the game. Get someone to sell their house."

"That is some kind of stupid." Dixon started for the door.

"Where are you going?" Preston asked.

Dixon stopped to pick up his radio from the charging dock and turned back. "I think you just might have earned yourself a real job, Mr. Farwick. I'll be back in a few minutes."

Chapter 79

Officer Dixon pulled his cruiser to a stop on the street next to Memorial Park. The events of the past few days had taken on a surreal quality. Most of his night work involved intervening in domestic violence disputes. Of course, there were the routine drug busts. Once or twice a missing person report. In 12 years with the department he only twice encountered an active shooter. Never once had he seen racially motivated hate crimes. He supposed that still happened in the South somewhere. But not here. Not in Florin.

Now, suddenly, it was everywhere. It showed up at school board meetings, graffiti in train stations and in underground chambers he didn't even know existed. Then there was this. Number 122 on West Oak looked quiet now. No one would guess it as a target for racial harassment.

Dixon stared across the street and shook his head. In front of the Faraj residence a large blue sign had been hammered down into the neatly mown grass by the mailbox.

For sale.

Chapter 80

Lisa closed the door behind her. The world seemed suddenly alive. Clothes. Desk. Chair. Poster with a folded corner. Plastic tiara on her dresser. Relics now. She passed the mirror and saw her own sad smile. Eyes red from tears. She knew this would be the night. Kneeling on the carpet by her bed, Lisa reached underneath and pulled out her scrapbook. Carefully she opened the brown cover. A single crayon coloring page slipped from its place. The princess looked up at her. Perfect yellow hair. Flowing gown. More pages—the ugly letters.

Lisa read them. Every one. She closed her eyes and saw words like tiny razor blades cutting her soul. Bleeding the ugly out. Letting more ugly out. She sighed and read the words aloud, settling into the song of hatred.

She listened to the words. New ones now. Other voices. Lisa looked toward the window and realized the song came from inside her. She rolled to her stomach and reached farther under the bed. Her hand returned clutching a tiny velvet bag. She petted the tender pile of the velvet smoothing it first one way, then the other. Fingers played with the black drawstring.

Lisa sat now, rocking the tiny velvet bag in her arms, whisper singing the lullaby.

"Rock a bye baby." The song of her own voice joined the song inside her. Today would end the torment. A palpable relief overspread the room. You'll make the world a better place when you leave it, it said.

Calm torment wrapped its arms around her. The words hurt good. Read some more, she thought. Read me to sleep.

She picked at the opening of the velvet bag. Tiny pills spilled out across the princess. Careful, now, she told herself. Don't lose any. Some pink, some white. Count them slowly. "When the wind blows." Lisa sang and counted. Counting and singing. Pink and white pills in tidy piles. Nine groups of 10. She'd been saving for a long time.

Lisa opened the water bottle with her teeth and swallowed them five at a time. Sing and swallow. The cradle will rock. The lullaby came from inside her again. Dark. Urgent. Grasping evil.

Lisa crawled up into her bed. She tucked a large teddy bear under her arm and put her thumb into her mouth as the lullaby voices sang her to sleep.

Chapter 81

Ashley lay staring at the ceiling next door. She wanted to feel happy. Wanted to feel excited about her game win. Instead she lay picking at the buttons on her nightgown and wondering what Jasmín found on the disk. Ashley stretched the gown to her mouth and chewed at threads in the button hole.

Her phone rang at 10:43 p.m.

Ashley fumbled under her pillow until she found it, pulled it out.

"Where's Lisa? Is she okay?" It was Darren.

"What are you talking about?"

"I can't get ahold of her." His voice held an unfamiliar edge to it.

"Maybe because she is sleeping?"

"Ashley. I've got an awful feeling."

Ashley was up and moving before he finished talking, infected by his panic. The hallway was dark. She groped for the knob and twisted it. "Her door is locked. She's probably just sleeping."

Ashley hadn't seen Lisa come in. Supper that evening was an independent affair. Ashley escaped upstairs as soon as she could to "do homework." She had tried to contact The Moderator, but he didn't respond. That was unusual.

"Her door is locked," Ashley whispered again into the phone.

"You need to get in there." Darren's voice choked on the other end.

Ashley felt a rush of adrenaline and goose bumps rise across her arms. She dropped the phone and knocked louder. She pressed her ear against the door and listened. All she could hear was the hum from the window air conditioner downstairs. Ashley swore.

Then she remembered the pin key used to open push-button locks. Her fingers slid across the top of the bookcase in the hallway until she felt the metal eye. She grabbed it, fumbled it into the lock and burst into the room.

Lisa was in bed. Ashley stood in the darkness of her sister's room panting for breath. Trying to push back the reasonless panic. Lisa's phone vibrated on her nightstand. The sound rattled her badly. "Lisa, turn off your phone," Ashley walked toward it. Lisa stirred. The goose flesh returned. The phone buzzed again, Darren's name flashing on the screen. It seemed like Lisa was shivering in her bed. Strange.

Ashley flicked on the lamp.

Blind white eyes stared at her. Lisa's face contorted in the grip of a convulsion. A thin trickle of blood ran down the side of her white face and bloody saliva bubbled up from between her lips. Lisa's back arched with the seizure; her fingers twisted into rigid claws.

Ashley coughed back grief and fear and vomit. She grabbed for the phone and shouted, "Call 911."

"Daddy!" The sound of her own scream frightened her. She couldn't control the shivering. She had to do something. "Daddy!"

She ran from the room and flew down the stairs. Her foot slipped and she landed hard on her bottom. Her dad stepped out of his office.

"What's the matter?"

"Help Lisa!" was all Ashley could think to say. The doctor. She needed the doctor. She wrenched open the kitchen door. The concrete felt cold under her feet and hard. She ran directly into the street, fighting to keep her legs working. The shaking threatened to overcome her. Several cars parked along the sidewalk like sleeping toys. Useless.

Ashley stubbed her toe badly on the curb, but kept going. She turned the corner and ran to the white and blue for sale sign. Her nightgown rode up on her legs, but she didn't care. Almost there. Lights from a car turned the corner and headed down the street. She reached the Faraj house, but stopped. She needed help. Lisa had to get to the hospital. Ashley ran out into the street, waving her arms wildly.

The car came to a stop. It was Dr. Faraj. Ashley couldn't speak. Sobs choked the words. "Help me." Suddenly she felt foolish, and pointed toward her house.

Just then the screech of sirens pierced the silent street and an ambulance rounded the end of the block and headed toward them.

"Get in," Adam Faraj reached behind him and opened the passenger door.

The car tires squealed away from the curb pushing Ashley back into her seat. She pulled down at the hem of her nightgown and noticed her legs still trembled.

"What's happening?" Dr. Faraj glanced at her in the rearview mirror as he accelerated up to the corner of the block.

"It's Lisa." Ashley felt the panic in her stomach, "I think she's dying."

"Has she been sick?" He turned at the corner and gunned it toward the rectory.

"No. Not Lisa," she replied. Sirens followed close behind. Ashley turned and stared at the red and white flashing lights behind them. God, please don't take Lisa.

The doctor pulled just past the front door to leave space at the curb for the ambulance. They were out and racing up to the house before the ambulance parked.

Her dad yelled from the top of the stairs. "Up here. Quickly." Surprise registered on his face when he saw Ashley leading a black man up toward him.

"This is our neighbor. He's a doctor."

"Thank God," Philip Blithe rushed them into the bedroom.

Dr. Faraj took in the room with a quick glance and saw Lisa convulsing.

"How long has she been like this?" Dr. Faraj's voice was calm and in charge.

"I found her just before I ran to get you." Ashley crossed her arms in an effort to confine the trembling.

"Does she have a history of seizures?"

"Never." Philip Blithe answered.

"Has she had access to any kind of pills?" Dr. Faraj glanced at the floor. A water bottle lay leaking next to a velvet pouch. He felt for her pulse and pulled up on Lisa's eyelids.

"Oh God, no." Philip Blithe looked at the doctor. "Please help her."

"Mr. Blithe, I have to know what pills you might have laying around."

"My wife takes all kinds of pills. Some for anxiety, some for back pain, some to help her sleep."

"Ashley, get me the pill bottles." Dr. Faraj said.

The emergency medical technicians filled the doorway, the room suddenly got smaller. "Make a space folks. We need to get in here."

"I'm a doctor." Dr. Faraj spoke without leaving Lisa's side. He pulled back her lips. The edge of her tongue showed, trapped, purple and bleeding from between clamped teeth. "It looks like we have a potential drug overdose. Ingestion of possible narcotic or psychotropic medications." He stood up to make room for the EMT's but kept talking. "Patient is seizing, has clammy skin, low heart rate, pinpoint pupils. Poison most likely ingested – no sign of venipuncture."

The EMT's lifted the blanket off of Lisa and slid her quickly onto the gurney.

Ashley burst into the room. "I could only find this one." She handed the pill container to Dr. Faraj.

He scanned the label on the container. "Oxycodone," he read aloud. He locked eyes with the EMT. "The seizure is asymptomatic for an Oxy overdose. It's probably a cocktail. Let's get her to the hospital, boys."

Chapter 82

Officer Dixon had almost reached the station when dispatch relayed the emergency call and indicated a possible suicide involving a white, teenage girl. He asked twice for the address. It couldn't be right. The ambulance pulled out of the borough office ahead of him. He hit the lights and wheeled hard around back the way he had come. The lights of his cruiser reflected off the black storefront windows as he accelerated down the main street of town.

No one was out at this time of night. Up ahead the ambulance turned onto South Market. The light blinked red ahead of him and Dixon slowed briefly to check for cross traffic before speeding through to catch up.

The ambulance turned off its siren after it made the turn and entered a residential area. He followed. His head was spinning. Surely Ashley Blithe hadn't gone home after he'd spoken with her and tried to take her own life, but dispatch confirmed the same address. Ashley hadn't seemed the type. The girl seemed confident, even casual, although she admitted to being nervous.

Officer Dixon pulled his cruiser up short behind the ambulance. The EMT crew was already on their way inside. The front door was open. Dixon followed into the lighted house. A woman stood leaning against the kitchen counter, stunned and unresponsive to his questions.

"Clear the stairs." The emergency medical tech at the top pulled the lever retracting the gurney's wheels. "On three. One. Two. Three." They lifted the gurney with the girl belted into place. They squeezed down the narrow stairway and Officer Dixon shoved the kitchen table out of the way to let them through.

It wasn't Ashley after all. The girl was older by a couple of years, thinner in the face, with brown hair, but obviously a sister. The crew maneuvered through the cramped kitchen and out the front door. Dr. Adam Faraj followed. He glanced at Dixon before following the EMT's.

Dixon knew that look.

Ashley appeared in the kitchen and walked over to her mother. "Lisa is going to the hospital. Are you coming?"

"I'll take you as soon as you're ready." Dixon said.

Ashley noticed him then. Tears flowed unchecked down her face.

"Is God angry at me?" she asked.

A simple question. Childlike.

"I don't know, honey, but we'll talk about that other stuff you've been doing later." Dixon put an arm around the girl's shoulders and led her out to the car. They paused to watch her father climbed into the ambulance. Ashley gave a little wave to her sister before the door went shut, cutting off their view.

Chapter 83

Jasmín Borbón slipped the thumbnail-size disk into a card reader the size of a jump drive. She sat down on her bed and plugged the white USB adaptor into her phone. In less than a second the phone recognized the new device, and Jasmín navigated to the file she wanted.

The micro-recorder must have worked, she thought. It was motion-activated, so she shouldn't have to watch an empty office. She leaned back against the wall and slipped her headphones on before she clicked play. She hoped to find something meaty to pass along to The Moderator.

The video blinked on with a bit of static and then a man and woman entered the picture. The woman was quite beautiful. She wore a simple blue or purple sundress; it was hard to tell because the picture resolution wasn't great. The woman came in smiling and sat across from a desk. She crossed her legs, adjusted her dress and waited as Ashley's dad sat on a chair near her. He wasn't as old looking as she imagined. Jasmín had never met the man. He didn't drive the girls to school, and Jasmín had never been to their house.

Jasmín turned up the volume. The poor sound quality made it difficult to hear. The two talked briefly about the weather before going into great detail about boxes of food or something they planned to deliver to needy families. They were friendly, but not intimate.

In fact, they barely touched.

Jasmín couldn't believe it.

Chapter 84

Ashley sat numbly next to her mother in the back seat of the police cruiser. They followed the ambulance all the way from their home. Late traffic pulled over to let them through. Ashley couldn't get the picture of Lisa out of her mind. She couldn't stop hating her father for letting this happen. She couldn't stop hating herself for playing the game.

Dixon pulled the cruiser around to the emergency entrance of the medical center and parked in the unloading zone.

"I hope everything is okay," Dixon said. Empty words.

Ashley closed the door after her mother climbed out, and the two ran in through the automatic glass doors. A television nattered away inconsiderately in the corner. Some judge was berating a woman for something or other. Ashley looked away.

A bored receptionist greeted them. "Can I help you?"

"Yes, my sister just came in on the ambulance. Can we see her?"

"What's her name?"

"Lisa Blithe." Ashley turned and stared. She hadn't expected her mother to actually talk.

"And you are?"

"I'm Elizabeth Blithe. Lisa is my daughter."

The receptionist glanced at the flat monitor in front of her. She pointed to the waiting area next to the television. "You'll have to wait over there. Triage will call us when you can go back."

"Please," Ashley interrupted, "we really need to go back now."

"Sorry, you'll have to wait until the doctor is ready."

They settled themselves in the waiting room as far from the television as they could. Ashley glared at the set and got up and walked over to it. She stared at the screen mounted above her head. Then she reached up to the outlet and pulled out the black cord.

"Excuse me, miss. You need to leave that plugged in." The receptionist wanted it on.

Ashley walked directly over to the woman and looked her right in the eyes. "We are trying to pray." She spit out the words one at a time and the receptionist backed down.

An analog clock on the wall marked the time as half past eleven. Ashley situated herself so she could watch the receptionist. The second hand moved slowly around the clock face, and she chewed on the skin by her fingernails. Her mother reached over and pulled her hands down into her lap. Ashley couldn't remember the last time her mother reached out to her.

Somewhere beyond the walls, a buzzer sounded. After a few minutes a cry rose from the emergency room. The hair stood up straight on Ashley's arms, and her terrified eyes searched her mother's face for answers. It was her dad's voice.

The sound rose to a wail. Loud and long and hungry. The sound made a word. One single word.

"Lisa."

Ashley knew then it was over. She collapsed, sobbing, into her mother's lap.

Chapter 85

The next few days blurred. The weather refused to weep with them. Instead, the sun continued to shine but the breeze was cool. The windows hung open to the living room where her parents sat together on the couch as people came and went. Ashley sat on the stairs.

Renee Hansel came, too. She hugged Ashley hard. Ashley was too tired to push her away. Too confused. The text message from Jasmín made the whole world swirl. Had she been wrong about everything?

Grief gnawed at Ashley every waking hour. When she slept, guilt crept in and haunted her dreams.

Chapter 86

"You knew it was me, didn't you?" Ashley asked.

Chase sat with her on the church stairs, out of view of the next round of people who walked stiffly in to visit their pastor. "No." He flicked a broken twig off his knee, watching it fly out onto the grass. "Well, I didn't want it to be you."

"I'm going to tell them." Ashley's voice was expressionless.

Chase didn't say anything. He broke another piece of twig and set it on his bare leg.

"I lied to you. I lied to everybody. You can leave if you want to."

"No." Chase just sat there, sent another twig flying.

"I don't know what's going to happen," Ashley said.

"I don't either."

"How can you sit here with me?" she asked.

He pushed his glasses up and his eyes found hers. "Because I'm your friend."

Ashley reached over and took his hand and held onto it.

"I'm scared." Ashley said. "Terrified, really."

Chapter 87

Ashley woke to the sound of birds singing in the tree out front. Sunlight streamed in through her open window. The air was cool. After a few seconds, the memory of all that happened flooded her mind, and she felt sick again with dread. She forced herself to get up and dressed. She decided to go to the police before the funeral. She was off school anyway, and Chase had agreed to meet her there. She wasn't sure how he managed to get out of school, but she didn't really care.

Flowers covered the kitchen table. Their beauty only reminded her of Lisa.

She slipped out of the house before her parents came out of their room. They were sharing a bedroom again. Somehow, Lisa's death brought her mother back from that far-away place. One day, maybe Ashley would figure that out. Now she couldn't imagine what life might be like without death.

Ashley walked across the street, turned the corner and headed down the sidewalk. The police station was only three or four blocks beyond Memorial Park, but she stopped by a blue-and-white for-sale sign. For a full minute she stood there, willing herself to go up to the door.

One step. Then another. She moved herself toward the house. Climbing stairs deliberately. Slowly.

She arrived at the door. Mrs. Faraj opened it before she could knock.

"Ashley. What a surprise. Come on in, honey."

Ashley just stood in the doorway. Her mouth moved, but nothing came out.

"Why don't you come in and sit down, dear," Rosalyn prompted again.

"I can't."

Rosalyn frowned. "Now, what are you talking about Ashley? You know you are always welcome here."

"No ma'am." Ashley looked at her feet. She pulled her toes together and folded her arms behind her back. Fresh tears. Regret. Shame. "I can't stay. I have to go down to the police station."

"Has something gone wrong?" Mrs. Faraj moved closer to Ashley.

"Yes, ma'am. I have."

Chapter 88

Flowers filled the church. Light filtered in through stained glass and warmed the shadows inside. Every seat was filled. A bunch of girls from Sutherland Hall sat somberly in a row, all of them dressed exactly alike in the tartan kilts and blazers with the school seal and the motto *Sans Peur* embroidered in gold thread.

The regular church members arrived and situated themselves awkwardly. Pastor's children weren't supposed to commit suicide.

Up front sat Lisa's coffin donated by a local funeral home. Apparently they always donated coffins for children. Ashley never thought about stuff like that before. The mirror finish on the honey brown wood reflected her own face.

A few heads turned to watch as an usher led the Faraj family to open seats on the right side of the sanctuary. Ashley noticed a few raised eyebrows before people turned back to the bulletin.

A black-and-white picture of Lisa smiled up from the paper. It included a write-up about her life. The paragraph was too short. What was there to say? Lisa had only lived 17 years.

Ashley walked with her mother to the front row and sat down. Her dad went up and stood in front of the casket. He turned and looked out at his congregation. People watched from their seats.

Philip Blithe opted not to wear his robe, but his clerical collar stood out white against his black shirt. A cross hung from a silver chain on his chest. He set his black Bible on the podium and opened the book. Paused. Looked up at the congregation, smiling weakly.

The sound of pages turning filled the silence.

"Our reading today is from the book of Ecclesiastes," he said.

Already he was having trouble. People shifted uncomfortably. Waited.

Finally, he began again, his choked voice barely a whisper. "There is a time for everything, and a season for every activity under heaven."

His voice stopped. Silence filled the room again. People looked down. Away from the coffin and the flowers and the grieving father.

"A time to be born and a time to die, a time to plant and a time to uproot, a time to kill and a time to heal," he continued, squinting at the words, "a time to tear down and a time to build." He stopped. It wasn't finished. He fought for control, read a few more lines, and stopped again. Pastor Blithe glanced at the congregation for help.

Nothing. No one moved. The reverend stepped away from the podium to collect himself.

Finally, a change. Dr. Adam Faraj left his seat and walked slowly to the front of the sanctuary. He paused below the platform, then ascended the stairs and stood beside the grieving father. He reached into his pocket, pulled out an embroidered prayer cap and adjusted it on his head. He put a finger down on the page, finding the place.

No one breathed. Pastor Blithe nodded slightly.

Dr. Faraj's deep voice cut into the silence, "A time to weep and a time to dance, a time to scatter stones and a time to gather them." He lifted his face and moved away from the book, speaking slowly from memory. "A time to keep and a time to throw away, a time to tear and a time to mend, a time to be silent and a time to speak." His eyes found Ashley. "A time to love and a time to hate, a time for war and a time for peace."

Chapter 89

Preston Farwick stepped into Chief Gregson's office and shut the door behind him.

"Ken said you wanted to see me?"

"Yes. Please have a seat." Gregson closed a file and set it down on his desk.

"I arranged a meeting last night with Mr. Kramer and Ms. Morrison. They're on the township board of supervisors."

"I've heard the names," Farwick said.

"In light of recent events and the information that you found, they have moved to make a preliminary approval for an emergency addition to the department. As a result, I'm happy to be able to offer you a full-time job."

Preston Farwick smiled. "Fantastic."

"Unfortunately, I can only guarantee the job for a year, but hopefully you'll uncover enough to justify the continuance of this position."

"I'll take it. The wife will be thrilled."

"Good. I was hoping you'd say that." Gregson stood and extended his hand. "Welcome to the force."

"Thank you. When can I start?" Farwick asked.

"You already have."

Chapter 90

The county court house dominated almost an entire city block. Carefully spaced gingko trees shaded criminals and victims alike. Everyone had to enter through security. The parade included social workers, attorneys, witnesses, but mostly, it seemed, the city's poor with plastic bling and tricked out phones coming to contest some petty offense or another. Drugs. Neglect. Disorderly conduct.

Court security officers mechanically funneled them all through. Scanners. X-ray for personal effects.

Upstairs, the Crime Records Department documented everything. Not that anyone really cared. Some records were permanent. Others not. Those lucky enough to be tried in Juvenile Court had files that were, officially at least, temporary.

A plastic pumpkin smiled from the corner of Sonya Hernandez's desk. She had picked out all the dark chocolate and left the rest for the other paralegals. The office didn't officially celebrate Halloween, but tonight almost everyone would be at the pub for happy hour. Sonya planned to wear a sexy little spider-girl costume she'd found online. She flicked through the folders on her desk, looking at silver webs on her fingernails. She didn't feel like working.

Her work tended to be interesting and made for great conversations at the bar. Most cases read like juicy gossip. Who got away with what. Of course, she never shared the names. Sonya logged on to the court intranet and pulled up the first summary statement she had to file.

She skimmed the report before taking note of the name. Racial threats. Intimidation. Trespass. Stalking. Sonya shook a spider-webbed finger at the screen. "My, my, Ashley Elizabeth Blithe. You have been a very bad girl."

She read closer. The child had received nothing but a few hours of community service and a lecture from the Honorable Judge Do-nothing. At least that's what all the paralegals called him.

Chapter 91

Farwick pulled his van into the garage and pushed the button on his visor to return the door. He sat in the dark, listening to the hot engine ticking as it cooled. The dog heard him come in and barked impatiently at the laundry room door.

His wife wouldn't get back from her doctor's appointment until later. He would surprise her with the news. No sense ruining the fun by calling it in.

Farwick pulled the keys from the console and got out of the car. He unlocked the door into the laundry room. A massive German shepherd bounded out of the house and ran happy circles around him before finally settling herself enough to sit and greet him.

Preston Farwick chuckled at her excitement. "I know, I know. You love your papa." He scratched her behind the ears. She whined with pleasure and followed him into the house. Preston Farwick pushed a button on the stereo in the kitchen. Chopin's Etude Opus 25 flowed like water over rocks.

Farwick turned to the dog and held up one finger over her head, "Beg." The dog immediately lifted her front legs off the ground and assumed the position. Farwick reached into his pocket and pulled out a treat. "Good dog, Cookie. Good dog."

The Moderator

For series updates, check out the author's Facebook page or visit his website at www.dwightkopp.com.

Other Books by this author include:

The Zambezi Chronicles: The Contract

Copyright © 2012 Dwight Kopp

The Zambezi Chronicles: Critical Fault

Copyright © 2012 Dwight Kopp

The Zambezi Chronicles: Cover of Darkness

Copyright © 2012 Dwight Kopp

Acknowledgements

Doreen (Doe) Kopp, Michael Long, Martha Squaresky, Jay Squaresky, Sean Reimer, Ashley Reimer, Sarah Donovan, David Curry, Tiffani Rooney and my Student Readers.